Pussy
Chronicles

FELICIA LEWIS

First Edition May 2016
Copyright © 2016 Felicia Lewis
Cover Design Copyright © 2016 Miss Web Designer, LLC

ISBN-13: 978-0692690050
ISBN-10: 0692690050

CONTENTS

LOVE & LUST EROTIC TALES 289

ABOUT FELICIA LEWIS 290

Visit Porscha Lewis's Website for the latest news and updates.

Website: porschaafterdark.blogspot.com

Instagram: porschaafterdark

Google Plus: Porscha After Dark

Twitter: @authorporscha

Facebook: www.facebook.com/flewis1985

DEDICATION

In loving memory of my aunt, Elnora Weeden. I write for you.

ACKNOWLEDGEMENTS

I would like to thank the following outstanding people who have come along this journey with me. You have put up with my ups and downs, my highs and my lows, but most importantly you stuck with me. Let's ride this wave to glory.

God, first and foremost, I thank you for this gift. Derrick Seaton, the love of my life, I never knew a love like yours ever existed. Mother, without you, I wouldn't be the person I am today. My bestie, Yvette Cotton-Taylor, and her hubby Punchy, we laugh like no other, and I thank god for you both. To my sisters Leslie Pollard and Darnetta Craig, thanks for always being a listening ear.

To my children whom I adore with all that I am. Tracee Smith / Jon Johnson (Future son-in-law), Teyara Smith, Stephan Smith, Ashlee Tillman, Rashad Plumpp, Taylor Littleberry, Corey Pennamon, and Jason Lee, you guys are the air I breathe.

To my grandchildren, Jaimare Wilson and Jasiah Morant, you are my light.

To my beautiful niece and nephew, Lavada Craig and Terry Craig Jr.

My cousins, Anttwon Weeden, Alonzo Weeden, and Willie Weeden Jr., I adore you all.

Grandmother, you are all that I destined to be. I miss you so much.

To my Uncle Arttours, thank you for being the dad I always needed.

To all my Weeden and Lewis family, you rock.

If I left anyone out, it is not intentional. There are just so many. I love you all.

Chapter 1

EVA

I am one of five badass women, and whenever you see one of us you see all of us. Now, in our everyday lives, people can easily assume we're in the corporate world and, in a way, you can say that we are. We run a prestigious escort service for very wealthy men and women.

There's Candace who books the clients, Desiree and Charlotte take care of all the entertainment and accounting, and the very feisty Latina by the name of Eva oversees it all. Then you have me, Samantha, who runs the establishment in the French Riviera. See, it was Eva who got all of us girls together to open and start the Pussy Chronicles. The name in itself is everything: an endless supply of ass on demand, amongst other things.

I met Eva in college and we just clicked right away. She always had a feisty demeanor about her, and always got her way.

The other girls came along later from different walks of life and now we're all inseparable. This was the perfect opportunity for all of us to make a helluva lot of money.

We have judges, cops, CEO's, and even the Vice President and President of a very lucrative Fortune 500 law firm on our list of clients. I'm not just talking about the people we service. I'm talking about the actual persons who work the establishment. People like to unwind when they come here from their everyday jobs. They feel they're in charge all day and just want some place where they can let their hair down with someone else in charge. That's just how bad all of us are.

How we're able to stay open so long is simple: we make sure we have all the top people in place. It's my mission to employ all the right people in the French Riviera, as well. We made sure the Captain of the biggest police station in Pittsburgh was a part of it all.

Captain Andrew Young calls in favors from time to time to ensure we keep our place of business legit. He has a very different way about him. He's the serious type, straight to the point, and isn't going to get caught up in a "situation." He's definitely made it clear that if it comes down to him or our club, he'll shut us down without hesitation. Captain Young's a sexy Italian, standing at six-foot-five with a bald head, goatee, and 330 pounds of greatness. He doesn't play, though, and nobody's going to fuck with you when he's around, so it's great that he's on our team. He's just my type of dude. I'd lie down for him any day of the damn week.

We also have Judge Frederick Malone on our side who likes to dive into some of the best pussy here at Pussy Chronicles. Fine ass men without women, or they have a woman, but can't be themselves around them, or sometimes the women just don't want to do all the nasty things a high profile working girl can supply. That's exactly why we employ some of the baddest bitches from around the world; they got their pick of the finest Crème de la Crème.

We didn't forget about our women—the men here are drop dead gorgeous and well hung. We pick exclusively from some of the most elite places around the world for our gentlemen, as well.

Our security team is the best the city has to offer. We always make sure we stay on top of our business and clientele. The things we've seen around here would make some people change their names and move to different countries.

That's just a few of the many things we have to offer for the protection we need, which goes so far and wide it's crazy. People, everywhere, want to come see what Pussy Chronicles is all about, and we're happy to oblige, as long as they pass all of our security analyses. Such security analyses include thorough background checks and screenings for major diseases. You're not allowed to come to the club with someone who already frequents it. We can't run the risk of someone being threatened by what we do. Meaning, we're making lots of deals when it comes to making our money. And believe me when I say that there are a lot of people with whom we have to split a piece of everything we make. It's fucking unbelievable.

We have this client in particular who comes through every two months. She's an executive of sorts and always requests two women and one man. We have to have her Loud on deck and, for those of you who don't know what 'Loud' is, it's a very potent weed that makes you forget or remember. That's all she wants. She told us that when she takes a hit of that shit it goes straight to her pussy and makes it wet and tingle. Sending chills straight up her spine, her clit stands at attention, and all she wants is someone's tongue licking and pulling and sucking the life out of her.

While she's rolling up, she has to have a chick between her legs sucking on her pussy, another chick sucking her breast, and the dude jacking his dick. But once she got that Loud rolled, it was on. She took that first hit, held it, and then blew that shit out. After taking another hit, she'd grab the back of that bitch's head from her breast, raise her face to her lips, and blow it directly in her mouth.

She'd tell her to hold it and then, before she let her blow it out, she'd push her head down between her legs and tell that bitch to blow the smoke in her pussy and suck her clit real hard. That'd make her cum instantly. Just looking at her when she does it makes our pussies wet. Just to see how she gets down when she gets high…

She'd have one girl eating the other chick's pussy, and the gentleman would come over and ram his dick down her throat. She'd suck his dick with all the tongue licking and ball sucking she could muster. She had an art of what sucking dick should be like.

That is what Loud does to her; it gives her the best damn orgasm of her life. See, to Jessica, this is the best time of her life, because any other time her life is chaos due to her demanding job. She's the chief executive in charge of one of the world's largest agencies. So you know her shit needs plucked every now and again.

She's also what you call a 'pillow princess.' She doesn't want to give head, just wants to get head. It feels so right to her. The way she explained it was that she likes watching girls get their pussies eaten while watching someone eat her pussy. She just doesn't think she can do the unknown and please someone with her nonexistent mouth skills when it comes to eating pussy. She knows how to work her mouth on a dick, but not a cunt. It doesn't give her a thrill to do that.

She also doesn't want to be in a bed, always preferring to be in a high back chair with her legs spread real wide, so she can see her pussy getting eaten correctly.

Even the owner, Candace, sometimes partakes in her chocolate delights. This client is sexy as hell. Candace knows she's never, ever supposed to fraternize with the clients, but does with this one. Her problem is that she's young and likes to party. I mean, she likes to powder her nose every so often, but it never interferes with her work. She's a very smart young lady who had it bad growing up. Candace never really likes talking about her childhood, but whenever asked she just says, "I don't want to talk about it." We just leave it alone at that point. It makes her sad to think about whatever she went through when she was younger, which is why I think Eva keeps her around, to keep an eye on her. We always want her to feel like she has family here.

It's just that when she's putting that White horse up her nose you can't tell her anything, and she spirals real fast and real bad. She'll be gone for days at a time, but still handles her responsibilities in waves from wherever she's at. It's just scary to imagine if she was in trouble we wouldn't know where she was or how to find her. Candace needs the Chronicles to pay for her expensive habits and her expensive lifestyle. I've asked Eva time and time again why she keeps her and, as I stated before, it's so she can be watched.

In the beginning it was her bank account that played a big part in financing Pussy Chronicles. That girl saved a shitload of money to come here from Iowa.

As I heard, she had the majority of the money to front the club. Just the thought of running her own business made her feel like she was doing something big that no one could take from her. Candace had something to prove to her family.

How about I just let you see how fierce we all are in our day-to-day business running of Pussy Chronicles. It will shock you, surprise you, and intrigue you with what we have been up to these last few years.

Chapter 2

EVA

"Candace," I say through the intercom, "Who are you talking to? We have a meeting in ten minutes."

"I'll be there in a second. I'm on a business call with the head of directors over at Universal. They want to see about using our location for a film project that's coming up."

"Okay, handle that. Just come in whenever you're through." Candace is real good at negotiations. She has a twist on words that will make you succumb to her demands. She has a very seductive voice and demeanor about herself that everyone seems to fall in love with.

"Hey, Desi," I speak into the phone, "are you and Charlotte ready for our weekly meeting? We've just got to go over a few things before shit gets crazy. Can you also let Frank know we'll need him and his crew in on this meeting as well?"

"Cool," she says. "I'll go grab both of them."

"Thanks. Damn, as I'm sitting here waiting on everyone to come to this meeting, I remember I have a very important call to make as soon as we're through." *Shit! How in hell did I forget about that call?*

*****

"I'm so glad you could make it to our weekly meeting."

This is one of my favorite rooms in this twenty-seven bedroom mansion. It's very tranquil and relaxing, perfect for our meetings. I specifically picked this room just for that fact alone. The walls are ocean blue with artifacts from the Egyptian period, so it has lots of cream- and chocolate-colored decorations. The office furniture is timeless pieces of cherry wood with large high back chairs. With surround sound inside the walls, there are three televisions placed high on the walls.

We also come here after a long day and watch all the newest releases sent over by Sony to review before they hit theaters. The windows are from ceiling to floor, and they wrap all the way around the office to bring in the natural sunlight. Yeah, when you come in this room, all your worries from the day just magically dissipate.

Frank says, "You know, this is the Pussy Factor. This time of day is always very busy. Myself and my security got to be everywhere at damn near the same time."

"Yes, sir, I do know what this is, I run it. I still expect for y'all to handle your business and be at these meetings on time. Handle all that extra shit prior to these meetings."

Frank sighs. "Well, we're here now. Let's get it cracking. What's up? What are we discussing this week?"

"Wait one second. What the hell is all that loud noise out there? Who is raising hell?"

"That's what I was trying to tell you," Frank huffs. "Some of the girls got into it."

"What are they arguing about?"

"You know how you ladies are when you get to borrowing each other's shit and not asking."

"No, I don't know anything about that, because I don't let anyone borrow anything, and I don't borrow anything from them either. Frank, just tell me who's arguing?"

"Those two chicken heads Jasmine and Frankie."

"Excuse me for a moment." I stick my head out of the office door. "Jasmine and Frankie, get the fuck here for a moment."

"What the fuck is all the yelling about?" I yell.

Frankie wipes her forehead as if bitching is a national sport that's caused her to sweat. "I'm tired of her ass always borrowing my shit and not asking, or bringing it back when she's through."

Jasmine rolls her eyes. "I borrowed some cheap ass eyeliner. I was getting ready to replace it, but she seen me put it back and got all defensive and shit."

"First of all, that's petty as hell." I feel like I'm talking to children, not grown ass women. "You girls make enough money to keep yourselves up with all the cosmetics you can buy. Now stop using each other's shit. It's unsanitary to be using makeup with all the dicks and pussies y'all have in your faces on a daily.

"This is a high class escort service, not a fucking daycare. Get your shit together or both of you will be looking for other employment. Do you understand?"

Both girls nod and mumble in agreement then go their separate ways.

Letting out a deep breath I've been holding, I say, "Now we can get back to business. Desiree, did we ever find out just how many clients our competition has? And who are they employing?"

"They have around one hundred to two hundred and fifty clients, so they're lightweights. The people they employ are not going to be a threat at all, simply because they're all fresh out of college and just barely learning the business. They're still wet behind the ears, so I don't know how in the hell they even thought they could be successful like that. I was talking to one of the young ladies over there and she was saying they weren't really sure how long their doors are going to be open because the cops keep running up in there. The owners are from Venezuela and have a shitload of money, but don't know exactly what they're going to do with it. So I guess they figured they'd try their hand at selling pussy discreetly, not knowing what's going on over here and that we got this on lock."

Charlotte laughs. "Girl, you can say that again. They won't last six months."

"As long as they just stay in their lane it should work out fine," I say. "Or until I run them out of Cranberry Township. Frank, I want you to shake it up a bit over there. If they get wind of what's going on over here with all this pussy and ass they may try and start trouble."

Charlotte says, "Do you really think they'd try something as stupid as fuck with us?"

"You know," I say, "You can never be too careful in this game. It's always someone waiting in the wings to take your spot. I definitely think there's nothing to worry about. We got this shit over here sewed up. Our clients are very loyal, and our girls and guys got it too good to risk going anywhere else but here.

"We got to make damn sure we're not caught slipping. We're all in the same business. I'm pretty fucking sure their asses are up to no good over there. Please find out more, and try and give their employees an offer they can't pass up to come over here and work. Only two of their smartest people will do. Trust me, the others will follow.

"Once they come and think it's all good, we'll get rid of them. They'll never be able to go back and work there again. Being that they thought the grass was going to be greener on this side of the tracks. No club in the surrounding area will ever employ them. They'll be blackballed in the industry."

Charlotte looks shocked. "Damn, don't you think that's kind of harsh?

"Look, it's either us or them; you choose."

"Chica, I choose us for sure."

"I thought you would." The girls and guys and I share a great laugh at their expense. "Don't fuck with us. It wouldn't be a pretty picture."

"Frank, how are we looking with things on your side?" I ask. "Is the fire power and pharmaceutical items at the drop location?

"I got that handled."

"Good," I say. "I don't want any problems coming at us unexpectedly. This has to go over real smooth for us to be taken seriously. The Columbians won't want to deal with us at all if we can't move this shipment expeditiously."

Frank says, "I'll keep you posted."

"It's very important we move on that ASAP. We have one more thing to go over, actually two. We just got four more high profile clients. We're not taking any more for the rest of the year. Our calendar is literally booked, and I like seeing that, especially for this time of year. We're not even at the six-month mark and we got our guys and girls with clients for the whole freaking year.

"I have something all of you deserve for working your asses off so hard and doing the damn thang around here."

Frank says, "What's that, boss?"

"Bonuses. I was trying to wait for Candace, but she must still be on the phone with Universal. They're talking about doing a film in our fine establishment." All of us give each other high five's. "I'll go over everything we discussed and give her, her bonus check when she gets through with that phone call. I don't think you guys know what this means if they do a movie here. First off, that will be big for Pittsburgh; it's definitely an up and coming city. That shit will set us up for a long time. Fingers crossed that she'll close the deal."

Desi says, "Don't keep us waiting. What are those bonuses looking like?"

Frank and Charlotte chime in with the same responses.

"Whatever they are, it must be nice."

Frank says, "Eva has been grinning from ear to ear all damn day. So don't keep us in suspense any longer." Charlotte and Desiree are looking at me with the side eye, waiting for me to say anything.

"Okay, okay, here you go. Frank, these are also for your security. How does twenty thousand a piece sound? Here is also another five thousand for your team?"

Frank says, "What? Are you fucking with us right now?"

"Frank, you know me better than that. I don't play when it comes to money. You guys earned every penny."

Frank looks up at the ceiling and slaps his hands together. I guess he's thanking God or something.

"What was that for?"

"I can buy my lady that ring I've been dying to get her for the last month. I just bought that house for us in cash, and that set me back a pretty penny. It didn't leave me penniless, but I wasn't able to do for her what I wanted and now I can."

"I'm glad to hear that. We've been pushing some pretty damn good numbers for the last six months and there's been no debt. Pussy Chronicles is in the green. We've been selling ass hand over fist and, with the girls and guys being able to see their regular customers more a month, that right there is where all the extra money is coming from.

"Here is each of yours. Go and enjoy. We'll conduct our end of day at 8:30, hopefully. I want us to get out of here early to celebrate the great year we're having. Let's keep this up and hopefully we can retire early. Y'all know I'm just bullshittin. I wouldn't know what to do with myself if I didn't have this place."

"Charlotte, can you make sure you inform the backup team to be here early so we can get the fuck out of here early?"

"Yes, I can do that."

"Let them know to be here no later than 8:15. Thank you all for your exceptionally hard work. Desi, come with me. Charlotte, make the call and, Frank, just stay on top of that situation. That has to run smoothly or it can mess up a helluva lot of money, and we can go down big time. Shit, we can't make money and lose it all in the same breath. That doesn't make any type of sense."

I have a weakness for pussy and, whenever I can make money the way I do, my panties get real wet and I need to feed the hunger between my thighs whenever time permits. My boyfriend Michael has no idea that I like pussy and won't ever find out.

He's a high profile attorney, and we look good together as a power couple. He also knows how to put the dick down in bed. Just thinking about how he pounded my pussy so good last night is making my clit throb right now. Damn, I need to get some lips wrapped around her quickly.

I have a taste for pussy every so often and, if he ever found out, it would crush him deeply. This is another secret I'll have to go to the grave with. He's probably the only man I know who doesn't think it's right for two women to go down on each other. I approached the subject once to see if we could have that kind of relationship. You know, I'd bring goodies home from time to time and he'd enjoy his samplers. Well, that was not the case. His ass almost threw up a little bit in his mouth when I asked him.

Michael said, "Honey, that shit is nasty as hell. Why would a woman want another woman sucking her pussy? That shit doesn't even sound right, especially when you got all this tongue to lap that cum right out your pussy."

I never asked him again. I knew I was going to have to secretly get my pussy eaten on my time with my girls. I'll have Samantha when she comes into town, but that isn't very often, so when she shows her pretty face I'll indulge in her sweet nectar and we'll have awesome fuck sessions.

When Desi and I get back to my office, I close and lock my door.

Desi says, "What's up with you? You've been acting weird all day. Not weird, just like maybe you have some important shit on your mind."

"I have had something on my mind. It involves you on your knees between my thighs doing what you like to do best with the soft folds of my lips. Bringing me to convulsions on your delicate tongue."

A smile comes across her face to let me know she's ready to explore my inner thighs with her pretty mouth.

"I been so fucking horny for you all day. I couldn't wait until I got you alone."

Desi says, "Now that we're alone, what are you waiting for? Get over there by your desk and spread that fat pussy, so I can show you better than I can tell you."

She grabs me by my waist and presses her pussy up against my ass. She unbuttons my blouse and plays with my breasts, sucking on my nipples so passionately. They get so hard so fast. I grind my ass on her pussy. The way she's squeezing my breasts is sending chills down my spine straight to my wet, juicy box. "I've needed this all day. Ah, yes, squeeze my breast. I like how you roll my nipples between your fingers. Ah, yes. Oh shit, you do things to me that no man could ever do."

"Do you mean Michael?"

"No, I mean no man anywhere."

She takes my hand and places it in her skirt.

"You feel that? You feel how wet this pussy is?"

"Ah, yes." I reach her juicy cunt and play with her clit while she squeezes my breast.

We undress each other very quickly to handle the sexual tension we're both experiencing. I love playing with Desi's clit. It's big and juicy when I suck on it, it's like sucking a mini dick, it was that fat. She likes how I rub her clit. I always know she's enjoying it when she raises her hands to the sides of her face and finger strokes her hair up like she's putting it in a ponytail. That face she makes is so enticing, that shit shoots chills straight to my waiting pussy.

I ask, "What are you going to do with this pussy now?"

Desi grins. "Let me show you."

Her hand travels down to my juicy box and finds my clit. The way she rubs it between her fingers has me going crazy.

Why in the hell does this feel so fucking good? I've been horny all day.

My eyes rolls up in my head and I'm in a total trance at what she's doing to my body. She's invaded my whole being with the softness of her touch.

She tells me to open my legs wider. "Oh, oh, oh, let me see that asshole." She bends over so I can make direct eye contact with her beautiful creamy ass. Her juices are so visible I can see them running down between her legs.

This makes me anticipate what's about to come next.

Desi demands "Stick your fingers in it and make me cum. Yes, you know exactly how I like it."

"No, not yet, I want to enjoy playing with you for a minute. Let me lick it. Ah, you taste so sweet." I slurp it up like it's the best ice cream I've ever licked.

"Oh that looks so nasty. That's it, spit all over it."

"Ah, you got my pussy so fucking wet. You got my clit throbbing really badly. I need you to stick your tongue on it while I'm sucking your pussy."

Desi says, "Come get it, baby. Open it up."

"You got a pretty pussy. Ah, shit, let me get my tongue right there on that fat clit."

"Yes, Eva. Shit, you suck it so good."

"That's it. Grind it all in my face." I take my tongue and go from her ass all the way back to her clit, not missing sticking my tongue up in her hole, so I can taste the juices as they come out on my tongue.

"Shit, Eva! Open your pussy real wide, I got to get my tongue all up in there. I want to lick all the sticky cum out of you. Put that ass up some, so I can suck your asshole."

She's pulling my head into her pussy real hard. I can tell she's at the point where she wants to explode. She looks so damn sexy grabbing her breasts and licking her nipples, and almost falling over from the way I'm making that ass feel.

I'm breathing hard, she's breathing hard, as I kiss and lick her all up the crack of her ass. There's no way I am going to ever give up liking pussy. I can't, it's too fucking good.

I make her lay down with the command to watch me as I put her legs on my shoulders, so I can caress her inner thighs by kissing them slowly. She squirms under my touch.

"Let me feel you like you always wanted to be felt with your husband." I lick her behind her knees, reaching up and massaging her clit as it pulsates between my fingers.

Desiree says, "Come here and fuck my face and ride my tongue. I'm going to put my fingers inside your asshole, so I can make it cream."

Just the thought of me sitting on her face, ass forward, with her tongue and fingers in my asshole, makes me almost cum. I assume the fucking positon the moment I take that spot on her face. Her tongue slips in my hole when she pulls my ass apart, giving me instant gratification. Unable to contain it any longer, I grab my breasts and squeeze my nipples hard, fucking her tongue like my life depends on it.

"That's right, fuck my mouth. Grind it just like that, baby. Yes, turn your ass over, so I can sit my pussy on your pussy. Let me feel that wet pussy soaking."

"Ah, yes, squeeze my breast just like that. I love the feel of your tongue on my nipples. You bite them just right." *I can't get it this good at home. That's why I stay so fucking stressed. I'm not even going to think about that right now, because the things that you're doing to my body are definitely not to be played with. Don't stop. Please keep doing what you're doing to me. I need this feeling to last me for a longtime.*

We both laugh at that.

Fuck, I love when you take charge and turn my body into Jell-O.

"Baby you're shaking under my body. You're about to bring me to full explosion."

I want to rock out on that ass. You got my whole body trembling. Don't stop fucking me. Let's ride this shit out of us. I want to cum all over that pussy.

"When you get ready to cum, I want to swallow it all."

How in the hell can we not fuck each other all day? Give me those pretty titties now, they're so fucking hard. I like teasing them. You just sent more chills down my spine. I like watching you ride my nipples with your clit exposed. Ah, yes, you taste so damn good.

Oh shit, girl, you literally take my breath away. I never work up a sweat like this, not even when I'm working out.

"Swallow my clit. Pull my ass apart. I want to feel all of you all over me. Wait, I need to put this hair up in a ponytail. I don't want anything getting in my way of fucking this ass."

I grin like a little girl stealing candy from the neighborhood candy lady.

"See how wet you make me?" Desi asks. "Every time you touch me you make me want you even more." *If I didn't have a family at home I'd want to be exclusive with her. What's so crazy is my husband has no idea I even like women. I actually don't, it's just something about her I enjoy. She intrigues me, and I don't want this to ever stop.*

"Desi, you remember this. Your pussy will always be mine no matter who you're with. Don't you ever forget that. Now put your mouth back on this pussy."

"Shit, baby. I thought you'd never ask."

I pant, "We're having such an awesome year with no problems, and you know how that makes me feel, so I need you to show me with your tongue how glad you are that I pulled them bonuses through.

"Yes, you know how to use your tongue. Slide them fingers in and out of me. Yes, fuck me. Just like that. Oh shit, you make me feel so good. Ah yes. I swear your titties feel so good in my hands. Just pump that pussy all in my face."

"My pussy is dripping all over your mouth. Bring me your pussy up here. I want to use the double dong, so I can see you lose your damn mind."

Desi is trying her best to walk straight; she kind of stumbles a bit with her sexy ass. Just watching her walk gets my juices flowing. She has the perfect onion shaped booty. You know she got that jiggle when she walks. Her perky nipples are standing at attention just waiting for me to wrap my lips back around them. I'm so glad its daylight so I can see her in all her glory with no distractions from the gloominess that nighttime brings. I appreciate all of her beautiful curves in this light. She has a way of taking my breath away. I wish I could give her what she wants, which is all of me, but I can't bring everything bad about me in her life. I'd hate myself if I brought any harm to her in anyway.

Desi asks, "Where's it at?"

"Inside the desk."

"In the top draw?"

"That's it. Bring it here and open your pretty legs. Your pussy's so wet."

Desi says, "Come kiss it if it's so pretty. Damn, French kiss it just like that. Oh, Eva, I can't take it. Fuck me now!"

"Get your ass on all fours. I want to stick my dildo in your ass and mine at the same time."

This shit feels so damn good. The feel of it vibrating in my pussy is so exhilarating. "That's it, fuck it. Oh, shit. Ride this dick. Do it, Desi, do it. Hurry up, turn over and suck my titties while I stick my fingers in your ass."

"Oh, oh, oh, oh, oh, oh, oh, I'm cumming."

Desi shouts. "Don't stop. Suck my titties. Play with my clit. I'm cumming right now." *As she gives me the best orgasm of my fucking life, I contemplate admitting that I'm in love with her. She'll assume I'm saying it because she was just rolling my clit between her tongue and sucking the life right out of me. She has no idea that when I'm lying in bed at night, it's her I wish was holding me instead of my boring ass husband, who doesn't know my clit from the hole in the wall. But you can't tell him that. He thinks he's the man when it comes to fucking me. I'm literally as dry as the Sahara Desert when we're fucking.*

I'm just going to enjoy what this woman is doing with her mouth, drinking every last drop straight from my core. "Haaaaaa, yes, that's it. Suck it dry."

I say, "Damn, girl, that was so good. I could lay here forever. Shit, we gotta go and get cleaned up before the cleaning crew gets here. It's almost time for us to bounce."

We start cracking up. With the feelings that take over our bodies, we can't help but feed our sexual hunger with one another. When that feeling hits, we get down on each other, our juices taking over our brain. We usually don't fuck in our place; it's very rare. We got to be walking around here dripping for us to give each other the attention we desire.

I go and find Candace to get her up to speed and give her the bonus check. To say she's ecstatic is an understatement. She laughs, hollers, and kisses me on the cheeks.

Flabbergasted, I stare at her. "Why are you so excited? I know this is a bonus check, but this is actually your average pay after two weeks."

"Girl," Candace says, "This came through at the right time, that's all."

"Oh, okay. If you say so."

If Eva only knew that I got myself in some shit, Candace thinks to herself, *I might not be able to get myself out of. I can't talk to her or anyone else about it right now. I just got to try and work this shit out before it's too late.*

Charlotte calls down on the intercom, "Judge Frederick Malone called and said he wanted to come through tonight."

I say, "That's fine. Just let the backup crew know because we're leaving at 8:30 today."

Charlotte responds, "Oh, he said he wanted to speak to you when he got here."

"Alright. Call me when he arrives."

Chapter 3

PUSSY CHRONICLES 1

Judge Frederick Malone delights himself with only the finest women we have in Pussy Chronicles, and we have some of the baddest bitches here. No one understands why he's single because he's slap-your-mama fine. Tall with caramel-toned skin, he's ripped. He is so damn sexy and has full lips, his eyes are like a greenish-hazel that are dreamy as all hell. His body's chiseled to perfection, and he has a six-pack with that V that leads down to nine inches of pure bliss. Damn, everybody stays wet when he comes through. He's a young judge, too. I think he's only thirty-six, so there are a lot of good years still left in that body. I would give him a run for his money, but I don't want to ruin what we have as far as our professional dealings are concerned.

That's why we were shocked when we found out he didn't have a woman. He's the epitome of a great guy, he just has a fetish that some would say is a bit strange, but fuck, that's who he is. He likes to have his women tie a rope around the base of his dick. To him it serves its purpose for what he wants, a fuck that will take him so high he won't want to come down.

While he gets his dick sucked, they have to pull it real tight, cutting off his blood supply. The girls always say that when he fucks you he goes for hours. He likes to keep the rope tied while he fucks the girls. Having them get into a doggie style position, he grabs their waist and, with perfect precision, goes straight up in their pussy until he feels himself touching the tip of their walls. He fucks that way until he explodes deep within her. He bangs and bangs almost to the point where he rams them. They more than likely can't take it, but they take the beating of their pussies because he leaves great tips, and none of them want to admit they can't handle him. He's very well-endowed, which is where his ego comes from. This brother is so damn fine no one ever bothers to say anything.

They just let him fuck.

There's something very peculiar about him, but you would never guess that. He doesn't say much. I assume the reason he's quiet is because he talks all day in court. He always thanks the girls for a great time and leaves them nice tips. We all think it's a little peculiar, but what he does is on him, and how he likes it is up to us to provide. Besides, he's one of the powerful officials keeping our place clean and open. He always keeps us updated with any news he thinks can affect our business.

"Hello, Judge Malone. How are you today?"

"I'm good, Charlotte. How are you?"

Charlotte smiles with that devious grin. "Better now that you've graced us with your presence. Hold on, let me call Eva. I know you wanted to speak to her. We have you set up on the fourth floor in the penthouse. Enjoy."

"Thank you, I'm sure I will. Hold up for a minute. Why don't you ever give me the time of day?

"You do know I'm married, right?"

"I'm sorry. I didn't mean to overstep my boundaries. Please forgive me."

"No problem," Charlotte says with a shrug. "It's nice to know you're feeling me." That man has no idea I would give him the business if my husband didn't know who he was. See, they play on the same green at the country club we frequent a lot. I don't do pressure well, so I can't even visit that territory.

The judge comes into where Eva is.

"Hello, Frederick. How are you?"

"I'm good, Eva. You are beautiful as ever."

"Thank you," Eva says, feeling herself blush. "You've always been the charmer. What is it I can do for you today?"

"I just wanted to let you know that everything is cool right now. You just have to be real careful."

Eva's heart begins racing. "Why is that? What's going on?"

"There's a good amount of drugs circulating through the area. I just sent two low lives to jail for twenty-five years because they were transporting narcotics all over the eastern hemisphere. But they aren't who we want."

The Judge reclines in his chair, casually slipping his leg over his left knee. "We want the distributor. We want the bitches that are bringing that deadly shit over here. The amount of stuff you're doing could lead us straight to them. I know you got that shipment about to go out. I need you to make sure it gets to where it's going, so I can make sure them bastards get what's coming to them.

"As soon as you get word, pass it to me, so I can pass it onto the attorney general's office. Intel will pass it on to the Feds and they will take over from there. We got to get the bad batch of Heroin off the streets that they calling Hercules. It's killing everybody in the 412 area. That shit is running rapid all through the North side and the Hill district. Just about everybody in the East liberty and the Homewood area is trying their best to get their hands on it, even after knowing it kills you almost instantly. You also want to make sure that what you're distributing is not in the realm of that fucked up shit that's being passed off."

Eva tells him, "Ours can't get mixed up. Our bags are stamped with Iron Man." With a sigh, Eva asks him the big question. "Frederick, if I give you them, where in the hell are we supposed to get our product from?"

The Judge waves his hand as if this fact is of no consequence. "We need this bust in a big way. There are so many suppliers in and around the world. I'm pretty sure you'll find someone else. You don't want to get yourself caught up in that game and it leads back to you.

"This is a major risk if they even found out I had anything to do with this. They'll come for me and kill me. Do you want that blood on your hands? We're talking about the fucking Columbian Cartel. They don't give a shit about what you're conspiring. All they want is their money.

"If they don't get their money, you know exactly what can become of me. Do I have to spell it out to you, Frederick?"

"Nothing is going to happen to you, I promise. I already informed some of the head honchos who deal directly with me and who's on payroll to make sure you're protected. You won't even know they're there. You guys just keep doing business as usual.

"Look, if you can just listen once and stop being so damn stubborn, all of this can just go away with a little bit of cooperation from you."

"Alright, Frederick," Eva says after folding her arms uncomfortably under her breasts. "I'm going on your word that everything will be fine."

"You have nothing to worry about. I promise."

Eva laughs without humor. "There's always something to worry about when you're in this deep. If they can't trust you, and you slip up one time, they come and kill you and everyone you know. That's some dirty shit, Frederick. You could've told me this shit when you first found out about it. No heads up at all. It's like you just fucked me raw."

"Come on, don't be like that. The shit hasn't hit the fan. We got you covered."

"Well it sure feels like it has. But you don't worry about if I get killed. My blood will be on your hands."

"I already told you there's nothing to worry about. Now let me get to my girls. There's something I need to get off my chest or, should I say, my dick." The Judge chuckles at his joke, but quickly sobers at the lack of humor on Eva's face. "Seriously, I'll talk to you later. I'll keep you posted."

"Enjoy my girls."

Chapter 4

EVA

I got a million things to do before we leave out of here this evening, Eva thinks to herself. I got this big party and, on top of everything else, I now got to worry about this damn shipment. What the fuck was Frederick thinking? That's the problem. I don't actually think he thought this through. I don't know if I can put my life on the line so the fucking feds can get their man and gain another notch on their belt so they'll look good.

No one will ever know what the fuck happened to me if I get caught. Shit, I have to think of an alternate plan.

I really need to run down the hall to Frank's room and make this call. I know he's making his rounds, so he won't be back up there until later.

Good, he's not here. I don't know why he doesn't do something with his room, it's so dark with all this black furniture in here. It's just damn depressing. Shit, I'm getting a call. I'm never going to make this call.

Desi calls to say, "Hey, Eva, answer your line, its Vicky. She has a request."

"Oh Lawd, its Vicky with her request. Put her through on line three." The line clicks and giggling comes through the receiver. "Hey, Vic, how are you?"

"Eva, I know this is last minute, but me and my girls would like to come through tonight and hook up with Scorpio. I told them all the little dirty tricks he can do with his tongue. How can I let them down?"

"I'll see if he's available. You know Scorpio's always booked months ahead of time." I got to get these spreadsheets done. It feels like I'm doing a thousand things at once, including answering these damn phones. "I told you before that when you want Scorpio to get that shit into me about four to five months ahead."

"Come on, Eva," she whines. "Please. It has to be tonight. I leave town tomorrow for two weeks and my clit is calling his name."

"Bitch please," I shoot back, switching the phone from one ear to another. "Your clit is always crying." Setting aside my frustration in the name of money, I take a deep breath and let it out slowly. "Let me see what I can do. I'll call you back in ten minutes."

"Okay, I'm depending on you to make this happen. Oh, did I mention I'll triple your fee?"

"That's what you should have led off with!" I shake my head. "That's the shit I like to hear. Give me ten."

Scorpio always has ten to twenty requests a day, so I have to keep him with a minimum of ten clients a week. Scorpio's fine at 6'2 with light brown skin and eyes that are a blueish green. He's built like the Rock, but he's a real live star here. This motherfucker needs security when he walks around. He was an exotic dancer before he came here to work fulltime. It started off with him wanting to pay his way through college, but when he saw the amount of money he was making, college got pushed into the distance.

I talked him into going back to school, explaining to him that he's young and his body won't hold up forever. He needs a backup plan, so he went back to school and got his Masters in Nuclear Engineering. Go figure that shit—the boy is smart as a fucking whip! He can manage the hell out of a dollar, but can't seem to get it right when it comes to his girl. He tries his best, but working in this industry is so damn addictive it's hard to get out.

Scorpio teases the ladies. He's able to make his tongue curl in such a way that when he gets that clit in his mouth he'll turn your world upside down. He'll make you want to leave your significant other. That isn't going to happen to him, though. He has a very sweet girlfriend that he loves with all of his heart.

There was a time when he was going to stop simply because he could never bring himself to tell her what he does for a living. That thought left his mind really quick when he figured out he wasn't the sit behind the desk type of guy. She's under the impression that he works for the firm and I'm his boss.

I check his schedule for today and see he has only one client left. These intercoms come in handy. Just the press of a button and it goes to anywhere in this big ass mansion. "Scorpio, can you come down to the main room for a second please?"

"Yeah, I'll be right there."

I got to get this phone call in sometime today. Got to keep up with what Candace has been up to. I have a feeling something's not right, and I can't keep my mind off it.

"What's up, lady boss?"

"Hey, I know this is last minute, but I see you have one more client for today.

He sighs. "Yeah, and I'm trying to get out of here to take my girl on a date."

"You have a client who requested you for the evening with a couple of her friends. They're going to pay you two times your going rate."

"Eva, not tonight, please. If I renege on my girl one mo' time she's going to fucking flip."

I would never do this for any other employee. There's something very special about these two. Their relationship is rare, and the way they love each other is priceless. Scorpio will do anything to keep his girl happy, and she's very attentive to his needs.

"Let me handle your girl. With the money you're about to make tonight you can take her and buy her a pair of red bottoms and a purse. I'll also promise her she can have you for the next three days next week. I won't book you at all."

"If she ever finds out what I do for a living she'll leave my ass for sure."

I'm in total disbelief that he hasn't shared with her yet what he does for a living. She might not understand at first, but she'd come around. Just thinking about his situation totally exhausts me. "Scorpio, how long do you think you can go without her finding out?"

"I don't know," he says tiredly, "but she's questioning me about my office down at the engineering firm."

"Scorpio, calm down. Do you see all of these papers spread across my desk? It'll be fine. You think you have problems. I still haven't made a phone call I've been trying to make all day. But don't worry, I got you. I'll help you with that situation. I have some friends down there who owe me a favor, so we'll get you set up with an office you can take her to."

"That's straight. Thanks, boss lady. You're the best man. I mean, woman."

I chuckle. "You're so stupid, that's never a problem. So will you hook up with the ladies? I'll tell them an hour max?"

"Yeah, I'll do it, but just an hour."

"Alright, you go get ready for your client and get some rest in between before Vicky shows up, and I'll let Vicky know it's cool."

I know she's probably tired of me going back and forth. We got so much stuff to get done, especially with the accountant coming in on Thursday. "Charlotte, can you get Vicky on the line for me?"

"Yes hold on, Eva. She's on line three."

"Hey, Vicky, great news. Scorpio will see you and your girls tonight. Bring only two, and his time is for one hour at the rate of ten thousand dollars."

"Awesome, girl. You always come through for me. I'll be there by 5:30."

Talk to you later. Have fun." Scorpio's about to run through these bitches' pussies like a fire hose putting out a mighty flame. I laugh so hard my panties grow damp.

With exactly forty-five minutes to rest up before the ladies arrive, Scorpio takes that time to shower and grab a nap real quick.

Now that I got that taken care of, I need to go check on that shipment. I need to run down to the wine cellar. I know Frank's down there handling some unfinished business. I wish they didn't have to be so damn loud. Shit, you'd think they were down here killing somebody, and all they're doing is playing poker. The unfinished business he spoke of is playing these damn games with his cronies.

"Frank, how's it looking? Are we in the wind yet?"

"Shit, man, you can't beat this hand. I got a pair of aces. Hey, Eva. Yes, we should be good. I haven't heard that anything went wrong. So far so good."

"I don't know. Sometimes not hearing anything is not always good news."

"Stop worrying yourself. If anything happened we would've heard something by now."

"Just check on it." Damn, Frank. How hard is it to just to keep me informed? "Put in a call ASAP."

Frank is totally in shock that I would speak to him that way. "Now listen here, Eva. I said that when I hear something, I'll let you know. I haven't heard anything as of yet. You need to calm down before your ass blow this shit all up in the air. I've never seen you worry about something so much as you're worried about this. Is there something you're not telling me?"

"No, there's nothing to tell you."

"Whatever you say, boss. I'll get right on it."

"Thank you, that's all I'm asking. You act like I'm asking you to hide a body." Frank is always so sure of his self. It makes me sick sometimes that he's so damn cocky. The one thing I can say for sure is he doesn't play when it comes to handling his business. I've never seen anyone handle him wrong. He has zero tolerance for bullshit.

His wife and kids are adorable, and I know his wife is scared for his life. She's told me plenty of times that she's scared one day she'll get the call that Frank isn't coming home. She knows she can't tell him what to do or voice her thoughts about it. When she met him, he was upfront about his business and that he wasn't going anywhere simply because this was all he knew. Frank's been gang banging since he was ten, and his whole family is made up of thugs and prostitutes.

He isn't stupid, not by a long shot. He could've easily gone to college on a full scholarship just in academics alone or even football, but he dropped out in his second year when his mother passed away from cancer. That tore him up. She was the only one who could've made him change, but when she died something died in him as well, and he has never recovered from it.

Chapter 5

PUSSY CHRONICLES 3

Here come the ladies. Look at them looking like children at Christmas with big ole grins on their faces. They sexy, though they came dressed in their short, black fuckem dresses.

"Scorpio, the ladies are here for you. You have an hour."

"I got this. I'm on my way."

Scorpio has on a midnight blue Givenchy hooded zip up sweat suit that compliments his deep ocean-colored eyes. He has the hood pulled up on his head. Damn, that boy is fine. With those eyes penetrating your soul—the combination of his eyes and that sweat suit and that damn cologne he wore—it's all perfect for what he has planned for his guest.

Scorpio goes sliding in the room with that sexy ass toned body of his. I swear it's like this man has music playing in the background when he saunters his way up to the ladies. He unzips his sweat jacket just enough to expose his well-toned muscled chest, He has his head down a little with the hood up high on his head as he lifts his head. The women go crazy over his baby blue eyes.

In his deep baritone voice he says, "Ladies, I want to thank you for requesting me for your evening of entertainment."

The ladies literally have their mouths open, but they're trying their best to refrain from snatching his clothes right off of him where he is standing. I got to give it to the ladies, they're sexy as hell for women of their age.

"Scorpio, you are so damn fine. I was just telling my girlfriends how good you are with your dick and tongue. Ah, shit, girl. That's the move right there with his tongue!"

He put that pretty grin on his face. He actually loves what he does. He likes bringing women to their knees and watching them succumb to his every demand. "You like that now, huh? Why don't you ladies get real comfortable and let's get this nasty party started."

With a sexy purr, Vicky says, "I thought you would never ask, Scorpio. How do you want us?"

As he starts to do a sexy dance for the ladies he's coming out of his clothes. "I want all three of you to get on all fours on the bed, booty ass naked. I want to see them titties jingling and those asses shaking."

Vicky responds, "Yes, Scorpio. Whatever you want? We're ready."

"Which one of you ladies want to come over here and suck this dick and make it twice as nice and hard?"

Monica is very pretty, with long, shoulder length hair. She's very curvy and petite, with beautiful chocolate skin. "We all want to come get on our knees and swallow your dick whole."

"Stop talking and put your mouth on it." By this time Scorpio has his sweat pants off and his dick is standing at attention. Shit, he made my pussy wet. That boy knows he's fine.

"Damn, that shit feels so good. That's right, swallow it. Suck it back and forth. You know how to give some damn good head, baby girl. Vicky, what's your friend's name?"

"Donna. She's the one who showed us just what to do with our mouths. How men like their dicks to be sucked."

"Monica, baby, you suck it now. Shit, you swallowed this shit whole. I feel my man on your tonsils."

"Ummmmm hum. Fuck my mouth, Scorpio."

"Yes, girl, keep going. Assume the fucking position and get your asses on all fours."

Donna moans, "Lick our pussies. Oh, Scorpio. Do it. Suck our pussies. That feels so fucking good."

I'm watching from the upstairs cameras. When Donna tells him to eat her ass, he does everything but eat her ass. That shit's funny as hell. He slaps it, he squeezes it, but under no circumstances is he going to eat her ass. I'm damn near crying watching him do the matrix moves on them. All the ladies are fine, especially being that they are all in their late fifties. You can tell they pride themselves on keeping up their appearances. They're real cougars.

Monica moans, "Yes, you're so good with your tongue. I'm getting ready to cum."

"Hold that shit girl. Come here and slide this condom on with your mouth. You do that shit like a pro. Stay in that position ladies, I'm about to come give y'all something real proper like. Who wants this dick first?"

Monica gets in the middle since she was getting ready to cum. Scorpio fucks her first. Her pussy's real tight.

"Let me grab this waist and put this dick all the way in you. Don't run now. You want this dick take this dick."

"My legs won't stop shaking. I've never experienced someone putting it on me like that before. You got a gift between your legs, young man, and I would love to experience that over and over."

"You can have this dick in you as much as you want. Just get in contact with boss lady and she'll set it up. Turn around and watch me fuck your home girl while you play with that clit."

"Okay, Scorpio."

"Donna, slide that ass down, so you can get some of this dick, but you got to put this other condom on with your mouth."

"I got you baby."

"Shit, girl. Sit and back up on this dick. Look at them titties. Damn, they big."

"Here, baby, put them in your hands and squeeze them real hard. You like to bite titties, baby?"

"I sure do. You can definitely say I'm a breast man."

"Yes, Scorpio, just like that. Don't stop. I want it long and deep. Oh yeah, just like that."

"Spread your legs wider for me, so I can get all up in it."

I see Scorpio peek up at the time, noticing that the ladies have about fifteen minutes left. So he's about to break her back in real quick, so he can finish and get the hell out of there. He's a professional, though, so the ladies will never guess what he's doing.

"Damn, boy. You're making this pussy scream. I'm about to cum."

"That's right. Rub that clit."

"I'm cumming." Once her spasms subside, she blows out a breath. "You're a bad boy, Scorpio. I'm going to sleep for a week. Shit, you wore my ass out. You got my spine still tingling."

"I'm glad you enjoyed the pleasure I brought you."

"I more than enjoyed it."

"Vicky, baby? You ready for this dick?" Seeing her nod vigorously, he crooks his finger at her. "You want me to tease that pussy don't you?

"I'm so wet," she says with a whine. "Look at my pussy dripping. Can you put your tongue on my clit and suck it real hard the way you do?"

"Spread them legs real wide so I can get up in there."

"Ah yes. Shit, that tongue. Do what you do with your mouth. That's it. Suck it hard."

"Put this condom on, so I can fuck you right now." She throws them legs back over her head, so he can get his dick all the way in.

"Shit, you're huge. Be gentle until you get in there."

"Damn, your pussy's wet as hell," he says. "You okay?"

"Rock that pussy at your speed."

He chuckles. "Let me know when you want me to take off."

"I don't care. I've been so horny for your dick all week."

"Donna and Monica, don't stop playing with y'all pussies until we all fucking explode. That's right, rub them out. Vicky, that's it. Fuck this dick the way you like."

"Yes, pump this pussy, you nasty fucker! Oh shit, Scorpio, yes."

"Vicky, I'm getting ready to bust in your pussy. You ready?"

"Yes, baby. Fuck me real hard right now. Bust my pussy wide open."

"That's it. Shit, I'm cumming, too, girl. Damn, that shit was fucking great."

"I wasn't playing when I said I want you to be my boy toy. I can give you the world."

"Vicky, what you have in me is a fantasy. If I give myself to you full time the fantasy doesn't exist anymore. So when you need that wet spot fucked, I'll be right here. It's always a pleasure and, ladies, it was nice meeting you. I hope y'all come back and see me soon."

Donna says, "Oh, don't worry about that. I'll definitely be back."

"Thanks," Scorpio says with a smile.

"Scorpio," Monica says, "You've awoken something in me that I didn't even know was alive, so I will be back to see you as well."

"Thank you."

Holding out her hand, Vicky says, "This is a little something for you. You did our pussies so right you more than deserve every penny. We will see you again soon."

His hand held to his chest, he bowed. "I appreciate you all."

"Enjoy the rest of your evening," Vicky replies huskily.

Look at Scorpio running down the hall trying to escape the ladies! "Eva, I am tired as hell. Those ladies worked the hell out of me."

"You're funny, but you handled yourself well. Well, this should make you real happy. Here is five grand. Not bad for a day's worth of work."

"Man, those bitches about to have me go get my drink on and take my girl to the dirty O in Oakland and get them greasy ass fries that come in that brown paper bag wit a whole hoagie. I ain't even playin, I worked up a whole fucking appetite fuckin wit them."

We start laughing hysterically.

"Something is really wrong with you, boy. I talked to your girl and she's cool. You go and enjoy the rest of the night and I'll see you on Thursday. You deserve it." *Damn, Scorpio, you made me hungry. I just might go to the spaghetti warehouse when I leave here today. Oh no, why am I playing? I can go for a fat ass corned beef sandwich smothered in coleslaw from Primanti Bro's.*

"By the way, the office is set up, so you can take her to your legitimate job. You'll go there on Tuesday and Randy will be waiting for you. You take it from there and show her where you work. That should put her at ease, for a while anyway."

"Thanks, boss lady. You're the best."

"Get out of here before your girlfriend has both our heads on a silver platter."

"See you Thursday."

We're supposed to get out of here by 8:30, but it doesn't look like that's going to happen anytime soon. *Shit, I still got to go to the ballroom and make sure the party plans are straight and talk to some potential clients.*

This is the life we choose, and I wouldn't change a thing about it.

Chapter 6

DESIREE

Samantha strolls through on occasion to see how the girls and I are. She's our international connect. One thing about Sam is that when it comes to her making money, she's great at it. She can sell you a mansion and won't give a damn if you can't afford it. As long as she gets hers off top, she's cool. Her conscience is non-existent.

She says, "Hey, Desiree. Have you seen Eva? I have some very important news to share with her."

"Yeah, she's down the hall in the ballroom getting ready for a big party we're going to have in a couple of days. What's up? Why you always sneaking up on us like inspector Gadget and shit?"

"Girl, what the hell is your crazy ass talking about? I own this business, too. I don't need to call when I got some important shit to tell y'all bitches. So just bring your ass along cause you won't want to miss this news."

As we walk back to the ballroom we see some of the client's doors open. We see women down between legs just sucking and fucking and getting their assholes plugged. It's always so hard not to go and jump in the middle and get our freak on, but we have to keep it professional.

We approach where Eva is when we notice a very sexy couple talking to her about something. I'm sure they're some new clients since I haven't seen them here before.

Eva sees us coming to her and wraps up her conversation with the new clients. She greets Samantha with hugs and kisses. "So what brings you all the way from the French Riviera to our beautiful city of Pittsburgh, bitch?"

You know when I got something big, I got to show up and show out. "I have some great news that I had to give y'all in person. We just contracted a multi-million dollar deal from a very wealthy client for the next year who wants to come through twice a month, and he is enlisting four of our most talented, gorgeous girls. We needed two from the French Riviera and the others from here. He just likes to watch."

She tells us he wants the girls to just do all kinds of freaky and nasty things to themselves. No touching, just watching the girls eat each other's pussies and use strap-ons with each other, along with other devices. As long as he can see that, he said he'll be a very happy man and a completely satisfied customer.

"He'll be here in less than an hour. I already got my girls set up in the penthouse suite. You, my darling Eva, just need to pick two of your baddest hoes and bring them to the room, so we can approve them all before he actually gets here."

Eva calls Charlotte, so she can sign off on the agreement and check over the girls as well. Charlotte's in the blue room counting the money and making transfers when Eva calls down for her. She lets her know what's about to go down. She comes upstairs to where we are and hears what's being said.

She says, "Shit, let's get this money."

We all agree, sign the contracts, and are off to get the baddest hoes we have.

Chapter 7

EVA

We have two women perfect for what we need to get this job done; they got that magic touch. Their beauty is astounding and their bodies mesmerizing. Jasmine has a set of 34DD and a nice, fat, juicy ass. Her smile is as pretty as her honey complexion, and chestnut-colored eyes. Her hair is to her shoulders.

We know he'll love her ass to death.

The other girl is Natasha, a red bone with a set of 36C's, a nice heart-shaped ass, and short, sandy brown hair.

He might just fall in love with her as well. They both have the love for a woman's touch.

Once we got the girls to the room and we were able to check out the choices, we saw that they were all equally as beautiful.

Frankie and Sabrina are exotic and dreamy looking, something that's seen only in photo-touched magazine like Essence or Cosmo, but their asses were real and untouched.

All the ladies are ready for the client waiting downstairs in the foyer to come up. I call down to Concierge, so he can escort the gentleman to the penthouse. When he arrives, us ladies have to contain our composure. He's drop dead gorgeous. We look at each other. Shit, he got my panties wet. I'm sure the other ladies are quite moist themselves.

We keep it professional when introducing ourselves. He's a very wealthy oil tycoon from Saudi

Arabia. I ask him if the penthouse is suitable for his needs, and he takes our hands and kisses each one of them. "Yes, it is as beautiful as the lovely women you handpicked for me."

Charlotte says, "The room is fully stocked with whatever your needs are and, if by chance you need anything that is not here, feel free to buzz down and we will get it immediately brought to you."

"Thanks, ladies that will be fine. I'm sure we have everything we need."

Desi responds, "Yes, you are fine with a capital *fine*."

"Excuse me, did you say something?"

"Oh, I was just saying here are the lovely young ladies you requested. Are they all to your liking?"

"They are absolutely beautiful. Thank you, ladies. I will let you know of my experience when we are through for the evening."

We turn to leave, but look back as he closes the door just to take one more glance at this gorgeous man.

What the clients don't know is that we have cameras all over our rooms. The whole establishment is wired for the safety of everybody. We get to the media room quickly to see what's about to take place, and we are so glad we did.

The gentleman greets all the ladies, asking them if they're okay and if they're sure they want to be in the room with him. All four of the ladies nod.

"That makes me happy. Why don't you ladies get comfortable on that great big California king?"

The bed's right in front of a beautiful picturesque view of the city that, alone, is enough to get a person in the mood for a wonderful sexual experience.

They do as they're told, as he tells Jasmine to sit by him.

We knew he'd like her. She always wears this incredible perfume called Armani Code. It also helps that she's drop-dead gorgeous.

She obliges and stands right next to him. The other three girls position themselves on the bed.

He says, "I want you all to get very nasty and freaky in a very sensual way." Jasmine remains by his side as Sabrina, Natasha, and Frankie get right to it. Sabrina grabs Frankie by the throat, pushes her down on the bed, and gets right on top of her. They kiss and start grinding on each other's pussies.

Natasha gets down between the two girl's legs and licks from the top of Sabrina's ass all the way down to Frankie's pussy. She spreads Sabrina's ass apart, so she can suck on her and get her real wet. Then she follows the trail down to Frankie's pussy, which we can clearly see is already soaking wet.

He turns to Jasmine and asks if she can sit in front of him and spread her pussy real wide, so he can see her play with herself while watching the entertainment on the bed. After she nods, he sits her down gently on a white fur throw that's on the heated marble floor. He tells her to arch her back, open her legs, and fuck her pussy.

He goes over to the cabinet where we keep all of the party supplies and takes out a very nice, thick glass dick to give her. He wants to watch her fuck herself.

She takes it from his hands and starts rubbing it all over her pussy. She then takes the tip, guiding it up her stomach, to her mouth, and starts sucking it and swallowing it. Then, she proceeds to try and touch him.

He tells her, "No, I came to watch you pleasure yourself. I'm enjoying the show. Lie down on your back and raise your legs. Spread them wide. I want to see you take that glass dick and fuck your ass nice and slow."

She starts doing exactly what he asked. He then turns his attention back to the girls and sees Sabrina eating Natasha's pussy, Natasha eating Frankie's pussy, and Frankie eating Sabrina's pussy. The girls are fucking each other with their fingers and sucking the hell out of their pussies.

We can tell he's amazed they're able to perfect an O position. Everybody is having a grand time.

He's truly happy just sitting back and playing it very cool. It's like he's watching an episode from Real Sex, the triple xxx rated version, while all this was taking place in front of him.

Jasmine's about to cum, but he tells her no. "Not yet. Fuck yourself harder."

She obeys.

She's ramming her asshole real good by the time she tells him she's about to squirt.

"Go for it, sexy."

She hits that ass in the right spot and explodes. Frankie comes down and starts sucking on her titties until she finishes. The other girls are about to cum as well. Sabrina tells Frankie to come back so she can finish sucking on her pussy, and Natasha wants to finish sucking Frankie's pussy. They all want to explode down each other's throat at the same time.

The girls are going at it, they're moaning and coming to the point of ecstasy really quick. Natasha hollers out, "Don't stop. Suck my clit. Pull on it harder. I'm about to cum down your fucking throat."

Frankie and Sabrina start shaking uncontrollably as they release their orgasms all over each other's mouths. Breathing heavily, they collapse side by side.

Jasmine asks the gentleman if he was pleased, and he responds, "I was most definitely entertained by some of the world's most beautiful women. On my next visit I will request you same four." He gets up, and says, "Until I return." He gifts all of them with diamond necklaces that have to be at least seven carats.

We can see how big they are from where we're watching.

Frank comes in and says, "Boss, I got that information you wanted to know about."

A couple of us jump in our seats, like we've been caught watching porn. Except, this stuff is better. Our panties are definitely wet.

Recovering the quickest, I ask, "Are we in the clear for the shipment to go where it needs to go in the next couple of days?"

"We're all good and in the clear. Jack is down there now making sure the boat comes in on time."

"Did you also contact the chief of police, just to make sure we stay under the radar?"

"Chief Johnson is keeping us up to speed and making sure everyone's in place. The whole process is going to run smoothly. By 7am our shipments will have made it into the hands of everybody who've made their request."

"Good." I clear my throat and adjust myself in my seat. "Just keep on him. We need to make sure our hands stay clean. If anybody, and I mean anybody, gets in our way, get rid of them."

Frank tells all of us to enjoy our evening and, "don't spend all that loot in one place."

I give him the side eye. He says, "Charlotte, I already know yours is gone."

Rolling her eyes, Charlotte huffs. "Boy, whatever. I do have my eye on something special."

"I know you do." He smiles, turns, and waves at us as he strolls out of the room. "I'll see you all tomorrow. I got a very pretty lady to get home to."

I wave goodbye. "Tell Chelsey we said hello and we miss her around here."

"I will!" he yells before shutting the door behind him.

I turn to everyone and grin. "Alright, you guys. Let's get ready to close the evening out. That was some great news for us. Our shipment's on the way and we have nothing to worry about. See, when shit is moving quickly and smooth, it makes our job very easy to handle. Candace, were you able to close that deal with Universal?"

"Yep. Someone from their office will be coming here on Friday to take a look at the place and tell us what they're going to be doing, and offer us a proposal."

"What type of movie is it anyway?" Desi asks, swaying back and forth in her chair.

"They said they're remaking a big time Mafia movie."

Samantha snorts. "Well isn't that just perfect?"

We all start cracking up at the thought of such a thing.

"I don't know about you girls," I interrupt, "but I'm so ready to get out of here. As soon as the sheik leaves, so are we."

Desi pushes herself out of her chair. "Sounds good to us. Candace, what are you doing tonight?"

"I told some old friends I would meet up with them tonight for drinks and dancing. I haven't seen them in a long time, so I figured I can't keep dodging them like I have been. Besides, I feel like dancing."

Turning to Charlotte, Candace asks, "What about you?"

"Well, the hubby wants to grab a bite and discuss his future plans for kids and shit. We can eat, but I am not thinking about kids right now, so I'll tell y'all how that goes if I still have a husband after tonight."

I say, "Girl, that man loves the hell out of you. He's not going anywhere, but I feel you about kids. Right now we just can't do it until we get through with this business. And who knows when this will ever stop.

Things are going so good we can't even think about stopping. Desi, you always got something going on in that fabulous life of yours. You and your husband are so perfect together."

"Not tonight, ladies. I'm going home to soak in a long bath and curl up with a good book, a glass of wine, and get some much needed rest."

Desi motions at Samantha. "How long are you staying in the Burg?"

"You girls sound old and tired talking that bullshit about going home and curling up with books and shit. Hell no. I'm here only until tomorrow, and you bitches are going to have to change all your plans. I was thinking we all go out and do what we do best when I'm in town, and that's party until the fucking sun comes up."

"Girl, that sounds good," Desi says, "but I'm dead ass tired and I just want to go home and get some sleep."

Samantha grabs Desi's hand and tugs her toward the door. "Bitch, you can sleep when you're dead. We're partying tonight."

"Damn, Sam, Michael was supposed to come over tonight."

"Eva, if you don't stop with that shit. You can see that man tomorrow night if you want to. His ass will be right at your door like a little fucking puppy ready to lick the crack of your ass."

"See why you always saying stupid shit?"

"You know I'm right, heifer."

"What the fuck ever."

Chapter 8

EVA

With a grand smile, the sheik says, "Ladies, I enjoyed myself very much. Please make sure upon my return that those four beautiful women will be available to me again. Each one of them made my dick stand at attention and my tongue wet as hell. With women like that, beating my dick is going to come natural, and fucking my wife is finally going to be enjoyable." He laughs.

He doesn't have a problem fucking women, he just has to be very careful. He's a very wealthy and powerful man, so he doesn't want the drama of just fucking with a regular bitch. He likes to have a different variety of women to play with, and appreciates the fact that this establishment has total discretion with whatever he chooses to do.

I say, "That won't be a problem at all. We're all so glad you enjoyed yourself."

The sheik replies, "Immensely."

He leaves with a grin. We wait until we see his driver pull off before we give each other high fives for another very satisfied customer. "That's the only way we know how to do it, ladies. Now let's pack the fuck up and get the hell out of here before something else requires our attention."

"Okay, bitches, enough with this shit. It's time for us to hit the damn town and party. Call your men and let them know you won't be home tonight."

"Samantha," Desi says, "You're going to get all of us fucked up."

Samantha just replies, "Candace's the only one who doesn't have a man."

Candace's mouth drops open. "For real? Y'all just tried it."

"Seriously? I'm here only until tomorrow afternoon. My flight leaves at four. Tonight we party. All of you can put your lives back together after I leave."

"Whatever, girl," I say. "I guess we're going out, ladies."

Samantha thrusts her fist into the air. "Yes, that's what I'm talking about. I knew you guys had balls."

Laughter erupts from all of us. We sure do. Our men are going to be pissed, but for tonight we rule this shit. Ha!

Samantha just wants to get her tongue in my pussy. I want to fuck her badly as well; we just never mix business with pleasure until the business is concluded. Once it's over, I'm going to have her or Desi's pussy all in my face. I just had Desi less than an hour ago. Now it's time for some exotic ass. Fuck, my pussy is already dripping!

We agree to meet up at one of our favorite spots at twelve that will give us time to go to our places and get showered. Samantha will come home with me, and the girls will go to their homes.

Samantha wiggles her fingers at everyone. "Alright, bitches, don't be late. See y'all in a minute."

Samantha and I decide to shower together to save time, but now we'll play for a little while.

She steps in and I step in behind her. I grab her around that tiny waist and press my pussy against her fat, yellow ass. I spread those cheeks apart and demand her to bend that ass over, so I can get my clit stimulated while she fucks my fingers.

I reach up on the divider to grab my glass dick, which is very warm. I put it in her mouth, so I can watch her suck it. She makes damn sure I can see just what that mouth of hers can do. She grabs the dildo from me and puts her back against the wall while she pushes her pussy out, ramming that big glass dick all the way in her. She's fucking herself so good, I'm dripping wet just from watching her. She wants me to rub my clit and squeeze my breast.

"Oh, Sam, yes. Fuck your pussy, baby. Yes, ah. You like to see me playing with my pussy? Yes, keep doing that. Let me suck that juice off your fingers."

Samantha's looking damn good as the water cascades down her body. She's staring at me deeply and licking the juices off my fingers from my wet pussy. She grabs me by the neck and sticks her tongue down my throat. That causes a tremor of explosions to run all through my body.

I grab the glass dick from her and turn her around, so I can see her spread that ass real wide. She starts moaning and moving her ass against my pussy. I reach down between her legs and feel how fucking wet she is.

I spread her pussy so the shower water can hit her clit while I continue to grind on that ass. I turn her back around and thrust my tongue into her mouth, then suck on her big ass pretty titties. Rubbing her pussy the way she likes, Sam begs me not to stop.

Sam says, "Oh, Eva, you got my pussy raining. Oh, shit. My clit is throbbing. Put your mouth on it." She pushes my head down until my tongue meets her clit. She shoves my face all in her pussy.

"You taste so good."

"Ah, suck it. Lick it. Ah, ah, ah, shit, that's it."

"Eva, please put your fingers in my pussy now. Ah yes."

I do more than that. I turn her back around and slightly spread her legs, so I can stick my fingers up her pussy and ass at the same time. She pleads for me to not stop.

Samantha says, "Oh, baby, that's it. Fuck me. I swear you're the only one who knows how to please this pussy right. Shit, yes, yes fuck me just like that. Suck my titties. Ah, bite my nipples. Yes that's it."

"Baby, we got to make this quick. We got to meet up with the girls in a few." She hears nothing I say, just wants me to fuck the hell out of her, and I do just that.

I finger fuck the shit out of that ass and pussy until she comes all over my hands. She grabs my hands while she's cumming, her legs shaking. She's quivering, and I can tell a dynamite of an organism's about to erupt from her body within seconds, as she's squeezing my hands between her thighs very tightly.

She brings my hands up to her lips and sucks her juices off. "You're so fucking sexy. Your pussy tastes so damn good."

We wash each other, jump out, and quickly get dressed. The way Sam looks at me is like she has something deep on her mind. I don't want to ruin the moment, so I don't bother to ask her what's wrong. After we had such an amazing time, why would I fuck this moment up? If it's anything serious, she'll confide in me, I think.

She always reminds me why I miss that pretty ass when it's gone. Pussy Chronicles has brought all of us girls together in the most sensual way possible. Neither of us ever knew we liked pussy until we got this place. With Samantha in the French Riviera, we know we got to make it memorable just because it will be a long time before we can do this again.

She's here only when something really big is happening. She sets up a lot of clients in the Burg. I love the fact that we all make time to take long walks at the point downtown, especially when the art festival is going on. We have some of the best times together.

Speaking of that, I need to suggest that we get a play in sometime soon. I think Madea is coming to the Benedum, which will be cool for us to do. Although, we won't get to take her out sightseeing this time, she's here only overnight. Shit, I still have to make that phone call.

"Sam?" I call out. "Can you please go and get the car? I got to make an important call. If I don't do it this evening it'll be too late."

"Alright, just hurry. I need a drink."

I found out some very disturbing news about Candace that I don't want to believe. I have to make sure she isn't up to her neck in trouble with some men she hardly knows anything about. I don't even know why she felt like she couldn't come to us before it got to this point. The things I have to take to my grave.

Ring! Ring! Ring!

He answers, "Hector, is your crew still following Candace?"

"Yes, she's got herself into some terrible shit. Eva, I don't know if we're going to be able to save her this time. You need to make a decision soon on how you want to handle this."

"Unfortunately, Hector, I still have to act like I don't know anything about this. Not even the girls can find out. It's for our protection that I keep my mouth shut on this one. If anyone found out that I had any idea what she was up to it wouldn't be good, and I'm not going out like that for anyone."

Especially when she's not thinking and trying to hide the obvious. Candace has no idea I know she met two of the lowest scum bags on the fucking earth. How she could get involved with Antonio and his boy Roman is beyond me. It pisses me off that when she gets high off that white horse she loses her damn mind and thinks she's invincible.

It's getting harder and harder for me not to slap the shit out of her, so she can wake the fuck up and realize them thugs mean her no damn good. They just want to be able to run trains on her and make her ass move their little ass drugs and drug money to Columbia.

That's why I had to come up with a scheme to try and catch her. The bonuses, yes, worked. I'll know how fast that money leaves her hands when she blows it all in a night with them fucking thugs. Those bastards are trying their best to come up with enough money to convince the Columbians that it wasn't them who got Sergio killed behind them drugs that he was trying to deliver. They know if they don't have their money them motherfuckers are coming for them at all angles. They're using Candace to help them get the cash they need. I just can't figure out how she's running it.

As long as Hector and his boys keep tabs on her, I'll know her every move. She better pray that she can deal with this shit on her own. I don't know to what extent she's involved; I just know that her ass has something to do with it.

Antonio and that bitch ass Roman are locals around the Pittsburgh North Side area. They want to be known as big time drug dealers. Which, in actuality, they're small time street hustlers. Hector keeps me up on game when it comes to the locals around here. He told me they're being hunted by some of the biggest kingpins in Columbia for fucking up a large shipment that was supposed to get delivered to another local thug by the name of Shorty. Except Sergio never made the connection. He got killed coming back from Aliquippa.

Talk around town is that they're trying to stay real low so their dumb asses won't get killed before they get a chance to get their money back. Problem is the low-life fucks are always trying to be seen, and right in the middle of things. Who in the fuck hangs on Franktown in Homewood if you're trying to stay low? I told you, their asses are stupid.

Supposedly, Sergio was their boy. The Columbians know exactly who they are. My friend Adrian said she just saw them in Arts, a local bar where everyone goes to have watered down drinks, a good time, and some of the best damn wings in town.

Now, somehow, Candace got her crazy behind caught in the middle of this shit. The Cartel don't play when it comes to their product or their money. Once they give you the product, and something happens to it, they no longer care about it. But you better believe they're coming for their money ASAP. I don't want to be in the crossfire when the shit hits the fan.

My business with the girls is going exceptionally well. I'll not let anyone stand in my way when it comes to getting this money. I love my little sister and all, but at the same time, if I got to deal with her, I will.

"Damn, Hector, I got to go. I was supposed to be in the club a long time ago. The girls are going to be wondering what's taking me so long. Stay on top of her and get back to me when or if something happens that I need to be made aware of."

Sam's hollering for me to get my ass in the damn car.

Chapter 9

EVA

I'm walking fast to get in my damn car. Sam's acting like she's going to pull off without me.

"Shit, you standing out here talking like we don't have anywhere to go, or our girls to meet up with.

"You know damn well their asses are not going in without us. You are talking all that shit. Well, let's go. I been in the car ten minutes and you still sitting here bitching."

As soon as we pull up we notice the girls.

Here comes Charlotte with her shit. "Where the fuck y'all been? We've been standing here for at least twenty minutes."

"I'm sorry, girls. I had to make an urgent call."

Now she looks concerned. "Is everything okay?"

"Yeah, it's cool. Let's do this shit, ladies." We're headed in to one of the hottest spots in Pittsburgh. My girls and I look so damn hot and, from all of the stares and catcalls, we know we got this shit on lock. The lines are long, and it's obvious everyone is pissed that we bypass all that mess. They stare at us like, 'bitches'.

A group of girls holler out, "Why do they get to go straight in?"

Charlotte, with her crazy ass, says, "Baby girl, we don't do no lines. It's always VIP for all of us. Get some know-how about yourself and maybe, just maybe, you'll be about something one day. Until then, shut the fuck up, stay in line, and wait your turn!"

We all bust out laughing. Now, we don't act like this on a regular. It's just when we all get together we get loose and have fun. Fuck what you heard, it's about all of us.

As we make it up the stairs, the owner Alessandro spots us. "As always you look simply marvelous. He takes me by the hand and tells us that our table is ready just how we like it.

"No worries," he says as he escorts us to our table. "Tonight it's all on me. You always take great care of me when I'm at your place, so tonight I take care of all of you.

"Ladies, this is your spot. Do you approve?"

Samantha sucks in a breath in awe. "You've really outdone yourself."

We have three bottles of Moet ET Chandon Dom Perignon and three bottles of Belvedere and Grey Goose. The tables are filled with purple, white, and red rose petals, gold candles, and a bowl full of condoms and dental dams for them bitches' pussies.

We have the best VIP area in the house.

Alessandro says, "If you need anything else just let me know."

The music is loud, the DJ jamming. He's playing just what we want to hear. We have a couple of drinks, smoke some weed and, after we get our head right, we are ready to get into a little bit of nasty.

Candace sits down and plugs her nose with coke. She's said it isn't a problem, but I'm starting to think otherwise. I won't bother her tonight with it, but we'll talk about this tomorrow.

We make our way to the dance floor. Charlotte and Desiree are dancing together, and Samantha and I join them. We're really getting into the groove of feeling ourselves. The liquor has us feeling right, and that purple Kush is on time giving us the ultimate high that we deserve just for tonight. Pussies are on fire. That Kush makes them drip. I don't smoke weed a lot, but when I do, damn, I be on some other type of shit. It's unexplainable. All I want someone to do is ride this clit out.

Samantha grabs my ass and pulls me into her. It feels good grinding on each other. I'm kissing her neck and squeezing her breasts while she slides her fingers through my hair and sucks and bites my nipples.

I say, "Ah, Sam, you know exactly what I like." I reach down and put my hand under her dress, noticing that she didn't put on any panties. I start playing with her pussy right on the dance floor. She's enjoying it to the point of ecstasy, getting ready to take over her body.

Samantha says, "Eva, don't stop. Keep shoving your fingers in my asshole like that. Shit, I can't take it. Ah, ah, ah, fuck me!"

She starts rocking to the music as I play with her cunt. Her head falls back. She grabs her breast, her pussy pulsating right in my hand. She grinds real slow so I can feel just how fat her honeydew's swelling up. We get so lost in what we're doing; we almost miss the attention we're getting.

A very handsome stranger is staring at us. We gesture for him to come over. We take over his body. He's so sexy, tall, handsome, and lean. But, then again, I can't really tell between the alcohol and the weed. We're surely floating, but the size of his dick says he's fine, and I'm sure Samantha agrees by the way she's stroking it.

He reaches behind him and grabs Sam's ass. His hand never leaves my waist. My ass is pressed up against his dick, and he's rock-fucking-hard. His dancing's good as shit, too. The DJ's bumping Drake's "Hotline Bling," and the music, and his rhythm has me in a sexy trance, so I can only imagine what he can do if we had him in a bed. We surely aren't going to make it that far. My pussy's dripping uncontrollably and I know Sam's feeling the same way.

I can tell Sam's ready to take this over to the table, the way she's sucking on the handsome man's dick says it all. I waved my hands so the girls will know that we're about to leave the dance floor, so they can come join us. They're having their own party.

Charlotte has a mouthful of Candace's breast in her mouth and Desiree's stroking another man's dick. She has her leg positioned where he can stick his dick right in her pussy. She's about to put a condom on him and fuck his brains out. Desiree's good like that. She can fuck you standing up with no wall for support. She's flexible as all hell. All those years of yoga really paid off.

Oh, did I forget to mention this is a sex club we're at? Pom Poms is very popular in the Burg. It's a place where no one knows you, and you have to be of the elite to even get through the door. If your name isn't on the list of invites and you don't know the password, there's no luck of you getting in here.

I laugh at the line outside. It's literally wrapped around the block, and they have no idea that they won't be getting in if they aren't on the list.

Alessandro makes sure he goes over his list of invites with scrutiny to make sure you're never there on the same day with other people you may've seen there before. He's open six days a week, and the clientele he has is from all around the world, so he has a big team to make sure everything is always going to go on without a hitch.

It's different from our place. Our place is more of a sexual hideaway, although people do throw parties there. We aren't known for a club atmosphere, but more for the tranquility and quantity of sex on-demand that's available. When you're at our place, it always puts people in the mind frame that they're visiting Madrid. It's relaxing and sexy, and it has those exotic colors of fall.

Not saying that our friend's place isn't, it's just different. Hell, we both sell sex and, one thing for sure, sex isn't going anywhere—it's here to stay. Besides, we can't really get down at our place the way we can here. As I always say, we got to keep it classy. Our customers can't know we all get down like that.

Now, our friend's club is sexy as fuck with sexy beds, chaise lounges all around, and a very big dance floor. The bar wraps all the way around the club. But you have to experience it for yourself. If you could ever get on the list of invites, I'd suggest you look into locating Alessandro's club. It's an experience you'll never forget.

As the girls make their way back to the table, Sam and I are already giving this complete stranger head together. His dick's big and long and it tastes so fucking good. I suck his dick while Samantha sucks his balls. He has both of his hands on each of our asses, finger fucking us so vigorously. We stop for just a second to acknowledge the girls' presence.

Sam begs, "Yes, don't stop. Your fingers are working the hell out of pussy."

Charlotte says, "Damn that looks so fucking good."

I moan, "It feels even better," before getting back to sucking the stranger's dick. We never ask for names simply because it doesn't make a difference. We aren't going to see him again.

He comes down between my legs and puts his tongue on my clit. I'm about to explode. His tongue is gold, slithering all over this pussy like it's a snake.

"Ah, ah, ah oh yes. Lick it like that. Oh yes."

I say, "Sam, come here so I can lick your pussy. Sit on my face while he gets ready to fuck me." She tastes so damn good. "Oh, fuck this pussy. Yes, shit. You're so fucking big. Pull my ass apart."

"Oh, Eva, suck it. Lick it. Look at my clit. Look how fat you got it. Get ready to drink my cum. Yes, here it comes. Oh shit, Eva, I'm cumming. Suck it, don't stop. Ah, my pussy. Bang the hell out of me. I'm getting ready to cum."

"So am I!"

The guy says, "Squeeze your muscles on this dick. I'm getting ready to explode all in you. Oh shit, here I cum. Yesssssssssssss. Fuck, that shit was good. You ladies sure know how to please a man."

Candace calls to Charlotte to come over and straddle her. She starts kissing her.

"Candace, I want your lips on my pussy now."

Charlotte stands up and grabs Candace's hand to lay her down on the chaise. They get into a sixty-nine position and begin to suck each other's pussies.

"Oh, Charlotte, suck my pussy. Yes, suck it. Oh, damn, don't stop. That's right, that's it, right there. Fuck me. I'm about to cum. Yes, suck that clit. Pull on it. Shit I'm cumming down your throat Oh damn; your mouth is fucking amazing."

Candace gets up and crawls between Charlotte's legs so they can tribe. Once Candace gets her juicy pussy on top of Charlotte's and their clits on each other, she's grinding that clit so fast and nasty on Charlotte's clit. You can hear the wetness that's coming from them both.

Candace moans. "Oh fuck, Charlotte. You're going to make me cum. Don't stop, keep fucking me. Pump this pussy faster. Grab my titties. Squeeze them. Fuck me. Oh, oh, oh shit. I'm Cumming!" Candace pushes herself up, out of breath. "Hold on, let me get another hit."

Charlotte pushes back from her, and then wipes the back of her hand across her glistening chin. "Fuck no, Candace. I'm horny as hell, and all you want to do is make your fucking nose happy with that coke shit. I had enough. Get the fuck off of me. That shit is going to be the death of you."

"Charlotte, I'm sorry," Candace says pleadingly. "We're having so much fun. Please come back and let me finish sucking that pussy. I promise I'll wait to powder my nose. Come on, don't be mad at me. I'll stick my tongue so far up your pussy you'll forget that you were ever mad."

Charlotte shakes her head. "You got to stop that shit. You sure know how to fuck up a good time. If I wasn't so damn horny I'd strangle the shit out of you. Now put your lips back on my sweet spot and make me forget why I was mad at you in the first place."

"Is this good, Charlotte?"

"Keep sucking it like that. Make me pour my liquid all down your throat. Oh yes, that's it." Her legs start shaking.

"That's it, Charlotte. Pull my head in and grind this pretty pussy on my tongue."

"My pussy's about to explode all over you. Drink it. Spread them lips, so I can see your clit stick out. Fuck your hand like I got a dick inside you. Here I cum. Get ready to swallow my juices."

"Oh, Candi, I'm cumming!" My whole body is quivering from her touch. I know she sees my eyes roll to the back of my head.

I haven't sweat like this in a long time. She really worked my body over. Just look at my hair! It's plastered to my face. It's going to take me a week to get my hair back to the way it should be. "Fuck, your pussy is fire. You do that to me, Candace. You my girl, you just play too much with that coke shit. Go ahead and powder your nose. You know you want to."

Chapter 10

EVA

I don't know what the little disagreement was between Candace and Charlotte, but I can guess it was about that fucking coke problem Candace has. They seem to have it worked out, since Candace's face full in Charlotte's pussy eating her like a champ, and Charlotte's cummming all over her tongue. Shit, that makes us get back to fucking.

Desi growls, "Fuck this ass. Show me what you got!"

"Fuck me harder. I can take it," she says.

He starts sucking on her breast and she doesn't lose the beat at all. She keeps saying that he got her pussy wet as hell. She starts playing with her clit, rubbing it fast, and sticking her fingers in his mouth.

You can tell the whole room's having sex. You know that smell when there are just bodies in the room exuding their senses, and it smells so good. Not musty at all, just sensual arousal in the air.

Samantha asks, "Does my pussy taste good?"

"Fuck yes, baby, you taste real damn good."

"Fuck me then. Fuck this ass while I play with this pussy."

"That's right, baby. Rub that clit. Come here, so I can suck on them titties. Your ass feels so fucking good riding this dick."

"Oh, baby, wait a minute. I want to feel that big ass dick in my pussy. Put it in now! Ah, yes, you got my toes curling. Whoever your woman is she sure is lucky. Your fuck game is on point."

"Eva, let him stick his big ass dick in your ass, girl. You won't be disappointed."

We give each other a seductive wink.

The stranger comes over and puts his dick in my pussy to get it nice and wet before he sticks it in my tight ass. I start licking Samantha's clit again. I'm telling you, sucking her clit is like sucking dick; it's that fat and juicy, and I fucking love it.

She's grinding that clit all over my tongue and it feels so damn good. I go straight into a zone. This man can fuck!

He stands me up so he can hit these walls right. When I tell you he's fucking me like I have never been fucked before, I can feel this man in my soul.

He grabs Sam and tells her to bend over so she can feel the power he's giving me. He gets her by the waist and puts his dick inside her ass. He's going from her ass to my ass nice and slow at first.

"Shit, yall's asses are so fucking tight. Buck back on me. Take this dick!"

"Yes. Your dick feels so right in me. Don't stop. I'm about to explode."

Sam's rubbing my pussy and slapping my clit, and I'm cumming all over her hands.

This shit worked out perfectly. Stand side by side with one of your home girls while a dude gets both of you bent over, and she's stroking your pussy while you're stroking hers, and he's in the back going from ass to ass. Damn. Trust me, it's a must. Just try it. I guarantee you it will be one the best fucks of your life.

Sam says, "Baby, I'm about to fucking cum." She starts throwing her pussy harder on him, bouncing that wet, juicy pussy fast on his dick.

He grips her waist real tight and shouts, "I'm about to cum right now!"

"Fuck, so am I. Fuck, fuck, fuck!"

We fall back on his chest, look up in his eyes, and say, "Damn, you were good, baby."

"Thank *you*, lil ladies. You're not half bad yourselves. I'll see them asses again."

We both say it isn't likely.

By the time we leave the club it's seven in the morning, but it's well worth it. We get back to my place and rest up before we have to get Samantha to the airport.

We wake up in just enough time to see her off and say our goodbyes until the next time.

Chapter 11

SAMANTHA

I catch my flight right on time. I always have a great time with my girls, but it's time to get back to my country. I can't stay away long. Alone, I run the whole organization in my hometown. It's not as big as what we have back in the states, but it's mine. It took me a while to get it just the way it should be. I hand-picked each girl and guy under my employ, and I promised myself that I would not let anyone interfere with what I am going to accomplish. I need to get back and make sure my ship is running smoothly just the way I left it.

Chapter 12

EVA

Candace, Charlotte, Desi, and I get back to our establishment, and it's back to business as usual.

Veronica comes down and greets us. She's my personal assistant. "Veronica, hey girl. What's going on here today? Or, should I say, last night?"

"I called you and the girls last night, but I kept getting yall's voicemails."

"Well I'm here now," I say with a sigh. "What's so important?"

Roni begins to tell us that we had a client who was getting kind of unruly with one of the girls.

"Jack was here, right?"

"Yes he was."

"He handled the situation?"

"Yes he did. But it was very strange. I was watching the whole act with Mike and the girls before it started to turn ugly."

Candace steps in. "What happened?

"Mike came in and asked for his usual girl."

Mike is another powerful attorney who frequents the club about every two months or so.

"I already have Niki in the room waiting for him, and I'm watching and listening. Niki asks if he wants the same treatment. He says yes. Niki plays the music and starts dancing seductively while she's stepping out of her lingerie. Mike gets up and stands behind her and puts his hands on her breasts and presses his dick up against her ass. She takes her hands and spreads her ass cheek's so he can fit his dick right between her butt."

Taking a deep breath after talking so fast, she finally turns to the control room and motions for us to follow. "Just take a look for yourself."

We sit down in front of the monitor that's paused on the video from last night.

Mike says, "You're so damn fine."

The girls and I get an eyeful.

"Niki, I like when you press your ass against me, it gets me so hard. Will you try something different for me tonight?"

"Yes, Mike. As long as it's within reason."

"Can we get the other girl I like?"

"Let me see if Cheri is available."

Where is this girl at? Oh that's right, she did say she was going to be in the theatre. "Hey, Cheri, can you come to my room? Mike's requesting you."

"I sure can. I like Mike." Cheri leans in conspiratorially. "He's very nasty, girl, and with him I know I'll have the best orgasm. My pussy's already wet just thinking about it. Let's go."

"Hi, Mike. I hear from Niki you want me here with you guys. I'm down and ready to play."

"I'm so glad to hear that. Ladies, can we get started?"

Niki gets on all fours and Cheri gets under her. They kiss and grind their pussies together real hard, their titties rubbing on each other. Cheri grabs Niki's ass and spreads it real wide. Niki pushes her ass out, so he can see her pussy hole.

"Cheri, play with your clit."

All I can do is concentrate on the beautiful oil painting of a stunning naked woman in all her glory that adorns the ceiling above us. Niki's taking me to new heights; feels like my body's floating. I know I'm coming close to having a powerful orgasm. There's nothing like having your pussy sucked by a woman.

Niki sticks her tongue down Cheri's throat. They have his dick hard as fuck. Cheri spreads Niki's pussy lips open. Damn, she's wet as hell.

Mike asks Niki, "Are you ready for what I'm about to do to you?"

"Yes, Mike, fuck me."

"Not yet. I want to try something else."

So we see Mike putting lube on his hand, and we know for sure Niki is not into what we think he's about to do. This can get really ugly if he even attempts to put his fist in her pussy.

He makes a fist and goes over to Niki. He starts massaging her clit. "Oh, Mike, yes. That feels so damn good. Keep rubbing my clit." She throws her head back and grins. "Yessssssss."

Niki says, "Stick your fingers in my pussy. Fuck this pussy good with your fingers."

And then, all of a sudden, he balls his fist up and starts trying to fist her pussy. At first Niki's moaning, and then when she realizes that he's trying to put his whole fist in her pussy, she starts yelling.

"Mike, no, that hurts. Please stop."

Grunting, he says, "Niki, I'm almost there. Just take it.

"No, Mike, it hurts!"

"Shut the fuck up and spread that pussy. I'm paying good money for both you bitches, and you'll do as I say!"

I'm watching all of this go down wondering where in the fuck is Frank or Jack?

"Mike, calm down, let Niki go. I'll do it. I like fisting."

"No, Niki's going to take this. I have something else for you to do." His crazy ass is just pacing back and forth, mumbling and shit under his breath. He's on a bad trip. Mike has never acted this way.

"Move your pussy up to Niki's face, so she can start sucking your clit. I want to see her tongue licking and sucking the air out that ass."

Niki's wringing and squeezing her hands so tightly I can see the blood draining from them. You can tell she is trying to keep up a brave face, but is going to crack any minute.

"Mike, you don't have to grab her like that. We're fucking listening. What the fuck do you want us to do? You see she's crying and you're making marks on her arm. Damn, what has gotten into you? I've never seen you like this."

With no change in Mike, Cheri tries a different approach. Slowly and calmly, she says, "Mike, take your fist out of Niki's pussy please. You see she doesn't like that. We can all have a pleasurable experience. This is not necessary. She doesn't like it, Mike. If Jack or Frank hears her hollering, your ass is going to get fucked up. Do you really want that life, Mike?"

"Man, fuck Frank and Jack. They ain't running shit over here."

"You need to think long and hard about what you're saying."

"Bitch, I know what the fuck I'm saying, and if you don't get your ass over there where I told you to be, I'm going to fuck you up, too."

What the fuck is wrong with him today? I have never seen him like this before. "I'm in charge and this is exactly how I want it. Now both of you motherfuckers better listen or I'll have something for that ass! Or both of you can be replaced with two more bitches who'll do as I say."

Jack comes busting in the room. "What's all the damn yelling? Why is Niki screaming at the top of her damn lungs?"

Get your damn hands off of me, Mike thinks. *Keep grabbing me like I'm your flunky and watch what I do to your stupid ass.* "Jack, man, she's cool."

You sorry bitch ass motherfucker, Jack thinks to himself. *I will kill you where you stand. Be the fuck still before I choke the life right out of your sorry no good ass.* "Niki, are you alright?"

"No." *Look what he did to my chemise. He ripped it right off of me. This piece cost $750. Who the fuck's going to replace it?* "I don't want to be here any longer. I'd like to leave. This stupid motherfucker has lost his fucking mind hurting me like that."

"Go," Jack says, motioning to the door with his hand. "We have another client requesting you. Are you going to be alright? Do you still want to work tonight?"

"Yes, I'll be fine." She wraps her arms around herself. "I just never had anyone treat me like that before, and no one is going to start now."

"Nicki, come on. I'm sorry, girl. I won't hurt you."

"Man," Jack yells at Mike, "Do not say shit to her. You already have done enough."

Jack goes over and puts his hands around Mike's neck. "You can't be rough with the girls. You know what we expect and that will not be fucking tolerated! I should fuck you up just on GP alone. You are a dumb fuck coming in here trying to handle my girls. You like getting roughed up, you little bitch?"

He starts his sentence, but doesn't finish. He has a bewildered look in his eyes and they're glazed over. His pupils are very much dilated.

Is this what you want, punk ass bitch? You want me to detach your fucking balls right from between your legs? "Man, get the fuck off me.

Jack, I promise you I will make your life hell. "Make me since you so bad. You like being tough with women. Come on, get rough with me."

"It won't happen again Jack." *Shit, man, I said it won't happen again.* "I promise I just wanted to try something different. Man, I'm high on X and this shit is strong. I went about it all wrong, man. I've been under a lot of stress lately and I'm really sorry for that. That was a real bitch ass move."

Cheri says, "Mike, I told you I would let you do it to me. I'm into that type of shit. Now, are you ready to have a pleasant experience?"

"I'm ready," he says. He tries to shrug Jack off him. "Man, get your hands off my damn throat!"

"Make me, you punk ass bastard." *I'm waiting to see what your little ass is going to do. I've been waiting for a good fight with all this pinned up anger. I want you to jump. Come on, bitch, jump.* "You fuckin' do some simple shit like that again and it'll be more than my hands around your scrawny ass neck."

"Shit, I come here to do the things I want to do because I can't do them at home. I got that worrisome job protecting these fucked up ass criminals."

Cheri says, "Jack take your hands from around his neck he'll be calm."

I'm not worried about his little sissy ass. "Are you alright now?"

"Yeah, I'm good."

Nostrils flaring, Jack says, "Don't try anything stupid when I remove my hands."

Jack's the truth. He's all of 350 pounds of pure strength. If he gets you in his clutches he'll snap you like a fucking turtle and won't think twice about killing you.

We witnessed him kill someone. It was another incident where this dickhead got off on beating his girls, and Jack went crazy. He beat the dude to bloody pulp and then got rid of the body with acid. There was nothing left once that acid ate through his ass.

Mike's still trying to explain his way out of an ass whooping. "It's cool. I'm not going to do anything. All I wanted was a fantasy."

"That's straight," Jack says with a dangerous hint in his voice. "You can have your fantasy as long you don't treat our girls any way you think you can. If I have any more problems out of you I'll come back and fuck you up. Do you understand?"

"I understand, man," Mike pleads. "Look, I'm just here to get laid. If Cheri will accept the fact that I was acting like an asshole and still wants to be with me, I'll be on my best behavior."

"Alright," Jack says. He turns to Cheri. "If you have problems, just call down to the security room."

"We'll be fine," she purrs, turning on the charm. "Won't we, Mike?"

"Yeah, it's cool."

"Carry on then." Jack nods to both, making sure Mike understands, with just a look, he could kill him. With a slow grin, he walks out of the door, shutting it softly behind him.

That big motherfucker really tried to kill me just now. Damn. "Cheri, can you come over here and put your mouth on this long, hard dick and make me forget about what just happened?"

"Yes, Mike." *He would've killed you without a second thought.* "I'd like nothing more but to come over there and swallow your dick whole. You're one of my favorite clients, and I don't want to waste another minute talking."

That's right, big boy, take my robe off real slow? "Ummmmm," Cheri moans long and deep. "Yes, baby, see how this works? It pays to be nice. I also meant what I said. I'm into fisting, so I want to see just how far your fist can go up in my pussy."

"Damn, girl. I knew I liked you for a reason."

Watch me play with my pussy. See how wet I can get. I want you to put your dick in mouth while I play with my clit. "Yes, that's it. Fuck my mouth just like that."

Shit, you can take a lot down your throat. "That's it, girl, spit all over it. Shit, you're good. Fuck, you're going to make me cum if you keep doing it like that. I need you to suck all this cum out of my dick."

Yes, I like how you go up and down and suck on it while you're swallowing shit. How do you do that?

"That's right. Suck it, spit on it, and slide your tongue all around the base. Swallow it! Shit, that's it. Damn, you can suck some dick."

"What's the matter, Mike? Why are you getting soft? What are you thinking about? You got lost in deep thought just now."

"I'm going to have to apologize to Niki. I feel bad about what happened. I don't know what the fuck got into me. I don't act like that. You know me, girl. It's been a hard fucking week and, like I said, I popped that X right before I got here. I just took all my frustration out on her and you."

Come here. Let me make you forget about that for a while. Do you like that? There you go. I knew it wasn't me. That's right; let it grow in my mouth. Stretch my jaws out.

"Oh shit, you sucking the hell out of my dick. Let me see you stroke that pussy. Yes, that shit is soaking right through the sheets. Sucking dick does that to you?"

"Ummmmm hum."

"Fuck! Get it; take it all the way down your throat. Damn, where the fuck did you learn that at?"

Eva made sure all of us girls were going to know exactly how to suck dick this way. "I was taught by the best."

"Niki's an awesome girl who likes to party. You were dead ass wrong with how you treated her. So yes, you most definitely have to apologize. She'll be fine, but she's pissed right now, so the sooner the better. Maybe when you come back she'll be willing to party again with the both of us. Now let me finish what we've started and then you can go and make things right with Niki."

"Come here. I want to rub your pussy. Spread your legs. That pink pussy is soaking wet. On second thought, let me lick it."

"I want to feel your fist inside my pussy. Please don't make me beg."

This is the best part. I don't have too many clients who're into fisting, so the excitement I'm feeling right now is making me shake with anticipation.

"Let me get myself ready to take your fist in my pussy. Look how wet you got me? I need you to start off by putting one finger in at a time and, once you got them all in, then you can ball your fist and start pumping this pussy like it's your dick inside me and watch me work the hell out of your fist."

She is taking deep breaths to prepare for what Mike's about to do her. She stretches her body and spreads her legs to accommodate his fist.

"Let me play with my pussy first, so I can get her nice and wet."

"Pull that clit all the way out. I like looking at how big it gets when it's swollen." I like how I make it throb under my touch.

Just the thought of him watching me touch myself is making me even hornier. I really like Mike and, maybe under different circumstances, we could've made this work.

But he has a fucked up temper, and I will not get caught up in one of his episodes.

"Oh, you got me ready to rain all over your mouth. Slurp up my juices real nasty. Let me hear it."

He literally has his mouth open with his dick in his hand. I can tell he's contemplating touching me or letting me finish what I'm doing.

I giggle because he looks like a school boy watching his first porn.

"Lie down on your back and open your legs. Pull your pussy open. I want to see my fist go all the way in."

"Oh shit, that feels so fucking good."

"Pump that pussy on this fist."

"My pussy is so fucking wet. Don't stop. I'm going to fucking cummmmmmmmmm."

Mike pulls his fist out real slow.

I know I'm beet red from what I just experienced. Getting fisted is something you definitely have to get used to. It got the bottom of my feet tingling and the inside of my pussy screaming for more.

"Girl, you got the prettiest titties I've ever seen. Cheri, shit, I want you to be my wife."

"Don't fuck this up by talking about that wife shit again. We cool just like this, baby. Come and fuck me with your giant dick."

"You like when I pound this pussy?"

"Yes! I can feel it. I'm cumming!"

"I'm cumming too, baby. Right now. Let's do it."

"That's what I call fucking," he says, breathing heavily. "I have to lay here for a second. Got to regain my composure after you fucked me like that."

"That's cool. Sit for a second, because as soon as you rest you need to go find Niki and tell her how sorry you are."

"I will," he says with a sigh. "I'm going to leave her a nice tip as well."

"Make sure you come back and see me," Cheri says.

"You're always going to be my go-to girl. Don't you ever worry about that." He pauses. "I want you to think about something. I can take you away from all this. You can have enough money for the rest of your life if you just come with me. I'll set you up in your own condo and you can come and go as you please. Just be there for me when I need you."

"That's something for me to consider. I don't have it bad here. Everything's on my own terms and the ladies make sure I'm taken care of."

"I'm just asking you to think about it," he says. "You don't have to answer me now. I'll be back in a couple of weeks and you can tell me then. I don't like the fact that I've been seeing you for almost a year and it's not just me."

"Hold on, you see a few girls here. It's not just me, this is my job. I wasn't your first pick tonight, and that's cool, but don't make it like it's just been you and me."

"But it can be me, if you just allow it to happen."

"Mike, you knew all of this when we started. Don't I make sure you always feel like you're the only one when we're together?"

"Yes, you do. But I can't help how I feel. I've fallen hard for you."

"Why? Why have you fallen so hard? Because I like fisting? Shit, I'm a big freak and so are you, but that's no reason to change the dynamics of this little arrangement we have."

"Look, I have to get back, so just think about it. Here's something for you. There's plenty where that came from. Bye for now. I have to find Niki and apologize for being an idiot. Again, just think about it princess. We could be great together, and you'll never have to see that side of me you just saw. I promise you that."

"I will give it some consideration. You have a great evening."

"I'm going to hold you to it. Good night again."

If that crazy motherfucker thinks I'm going to give up what I got going on here he got another thing coming. Shit, he got that bomb dick though. But it ain't that good where I'm going to give up three stacks a week. I guess I made my decision.

"Sorry, Mike"

Chapter 13

CANDACE

If any one of my girlfriends ever finds out what mess I got my life into, things will never be the same.

It all started out innocent enough. I can't even recall when it got this bad. All I do is wish I would've never met them street ass hustlers.

One night of fun, fucking, and blowing coke started this never-ending mess.

Shit! What am I going to do? I'm moving illegal money through our club. I sit here contemplating if I should just tell the girls. How in the hell am I going to get out of this mess I created for myself? Lord, if you see me through, I promise I'll make a bigger difference in my life.

At least I wouldn't be deceiving them any longer. Fuck, I can't! I would not hear the end of it from Eva, and the girls would just follow suit and tell me what a fool I was for getting involved with them. The shit I went through with my family was enough to last me a lifetime. I will never let anyone think they got the better of me. I got to handle this shit on my own.

I know for sure Charlotte and Desi wouldn't let it go. It'd be constant nagging. How could I've been so stupid? Candace, wake the fuck up, girl. You're in this world alone. You got to make a place where no one knows who you are, so just do what you have to do to survive. Whatever the fuck that means.

Roman and Antonio promised it would be only once or twice. I wouldn't have to keep moving their drug money. Well, for the last year, I'm still running this shit through our club. If they don't pay up soon, it's going to be hell for all of us.

There's something weird about this that I don't understand. The Columbians gave them only a few weeks to pay up, so they say, and when that didn't happen they said they extended their time to get them all their money. They also stopped looking for Sergio's killers. I need to find out if all this time I've been getting played.

But if I was, where the fuck has all the money been going? Things are getting intense around here. I don't know how much longer I'll be able to hide this secret. The sooner I get answers to all these unanswered questions maybe, just maybe, that will be my way out of this shit.

I got to try and get some rest. I have a very busy day.

"Antonio, man, we got to get up with Candace to make sure she was able to come up on that loot."

"Shit, man, give that bitch a call. She's been MIA for a minute. Said she was going to be visiting family here in the A. If that coke head bitch is here, we going to see her."

Ring! Ring! Ring! Ring! Ring!

"Candace? Damn, what you doing? Where you at, girl?"

"Who is this?"

"Roman. Stop acting like you don't know my voice."

"Boy, its four in the morning. I wouldn't know my mama's voice this early. What's up, Roman? I'm trying to sleep. Why are you calling me? Shit, the birds aren't even chirping yet."

"Girl, stop acting like you're not up this early putting that white shit all up in your nose. Anyway, where you at?"

"I'm in Atlanta."

"Cool, so are me and Antonio. We need to link up ASAP."

"What for? I'll see you fools when we get back to the Burg."

"Not going to work. We need to meet tomorrow night."

"What's this about, Roman?"

"I don't want to talk on these phone lines. Everybody be listening and shit. Just meet us tomorrow night."

"Okay, I can do that. Where do you want to meet?

"How about that spot in Austell called the Blue Bar?"

"I can be there. What time? You know I got to get back to the Burg tomorrow."

"Man, fuck Pittsburgh right now. We got to make sure this shit is straight before you do anything."

"Hold up, Roman. I'm doing you guys a favor. I got a business to run. Man, I swear I wish I would've never got involved with y'all asses."

"Well you did. You shouldn't have had such a sweet tooth for that cotton candy. Your ass wouldn't have been so quick to fuck. Now I say that to say this: have your tired ass at the Blue Bar, or else."

"Or else what, Roman? Let me guess, you going to kill me. Stop fucking threatening me."

"Listen, bitch. You are not going to fuck this up. Meet us at ten. Be there, and if you're not, your stupid ass will be sorry."

Chapter 14

CANDACE

I'm already fucking sorry. These dirty dick motherfuckers get on my last damn nerve. How the fuck they know about that spot in Austell? That right there is where I go to get my shit. As soon as you hit the door on a Friday night you know DJTEFLONONTHA1 is going to be in there jamming. He's one of the dopest DJ's in the A. If y'all could afford him, I guarantee you he'll have your function turnt all the way the hell up.

The owners are some of the nicest people you'll ever want to meet. Fuck, I hope them two bastards don't start nothing in their bar. I'll be so fucking embarrassed.

I need to give my girl the heads up before I get there, so she'll know what could possibly go down.

"I'll be there," I say with a sigh into the phone. "Is there anything else I can do for you?"

"Yeah, how about you come let us bust a nut all in your mouth?"

"Good night. I'll see your grimy asses tomorrow."

Meeting Antonio and Roman is totally one of the biggest mistakes of my life. I was sitting at the Shamrock, a little bar on the Northside, minding my business one night, when I hear, "Damn, you fine as hell."

When I noticed the two guys, I was a little tipsy, but not too drunk not to realize that they were fine as hell. The taller one had the whitest teeth and his chocolate skin mesmerized me. His body was nicely toned, and I could tell by the way his sweats were fitting, and that dick print, was giving me life. His friend was sexy, a fine ass white boy. He put me in mind of that Tatum boy. "Well thank you," I replied, batting my lashes. "I'm Candace."

"I'm Antonio and this is my boy Roman."

"What're you trying to get into tonight, pretty lady?"

"I just came to listen to some good music and dance, and then go home, curl up, and watch some Netflix." *I wasn't planning anything too big tonight I got to get up early in the morning.*

"Are you doing that by yourself?" He sounded surprised.

"That was the plan."

"You want some company?"

"Naw, that's cool. I'm just going to grab a drink and chill for a second."

"Oh, it's like that?"

I rolled my eyes. "I don't even know y'all and you think I'm just going to invite you back to my house?"

"Hey, why don't you go in the restroom and get some of this? It's fire."

"I don't do that shit."

"Lil lady, you've been sniffing you nose for the past five minutes, and not like in an 'I got a cold type of way.'"

"Stop playing and take this shit," Roman said. "We'll be right here when you get back."

"Whatever, man. Give it to me." *These motherfuckers don't know I'm a G when it comes to me getting my nose right.*

I know they're looking at me. I feel them burning a hole straight through my ass. I'm so glad I decided to wear my True Religion jeans. They fit my fat ass perfectly. I make sure I put an extra jiggle in my walk.

Oh, thank goodness no one is in here. I lock the door and giggle like a little girl about to open up a giant present.

Let me see what this shit is about. Perfect.

I set my shit up right on the silver ledge and got out my fifty dollar bill, rolled it up, and placed it to my nose.

Fuck, what if this is dope? I should've asked. Naw, they don't look like they snort dope. Shit, I'm going to have to just take that chance. I need this shit right now in the worse way.

I sniff both lines within seconds.

Damn, this shit is fire. Naw, this ain't dope. It's that good coco.

It makes me throw my head back, turn my neck side to side, grab my breasts, and slide my hands between my wet pussy. That shit went right to my clit.

Okay, one more line, they won't miss it.

Shit, this is good. It made me do a little happy dance. *Now I got to get some more.*

As I stare at myself in the mirror, I start getting flashbacks of my childhood. It feels like someone had just slapped me in my face.

My brothers and father were so cruel to me. I was my mother's only daughter, how could they have done those things to me? Late at night, my older brother would come in my room and touch me in places where a little girl should never be touched, and then threaten me that if I told, he would kill me. I was only nine. That scared the shit out of me. My other brother caught him one night and tried to stop him, but Jackson beat his ass and he never tried to stop him again.

My father would drink every day while my mother worked nights. *Oh god, daddy, how could you have hurt me the way you did? You're not supposed to force your little girl, your own blood daughter, to suck your dick. That's not right.*

My mother was so caught up in her life that she had no time to pay attention to me, or what I needed. I made a promise that as soon as I was able to get the fuck out of there I would. This happened every day for years. I went to college and never looked back.

My brothers tried to find me, as well as my mother after my father died. I didn't care for any of them. They could all drop dead for all I cared. I'm now in this endless world of destruction and I don't know how to stop it from spinning. I don't trust anyone. I've never been in a committed relationship. My mind's all fucked, and I would never bring a child in this cruel, fucked up world we live in. My childhood was pure hell. I wouldn't ever subject another human being to the torture that I experienced.

"Stop it, Candace, get over it," I tell my mirror self. "You're safe. Shake it off and get back out there to your newfound friends. And get some more stuff. It'll make all your worries go away."

I go back to my table and Antonio's all in my damn business. I should've known his sorry ass was trouble.

"Damn, baby, did you do it all?"

"No I didn't. I would like to get some of that. How much? An eight ball would be good. That'll last me all night.

"Girl, an eight ball ain't shit. We got more where that came from. Just stick with us. You down?"

"Well, y'all don't look like killers or anything. I guess we can party together."

"For you, pretty lady, we'll give you what you want. This shit is plentiful. You don't need to worry about that. We can party for a week if that's what you want to do."

"I just want to buy some. So tell me how much. Money's not an issue."

"We got you. We don't want your money. Let's just get out of here so we can party right."

"Let me finish my drink. I got a hotel downtown. We can go there and party and dance. Shake some shit up tonight in the Burg."

If these motherfuckers think I'm taking them back to my crib, they have another thing coming.

"Okay, cool. Let me grab my friend and we can bounce."

"Roman, man, let's go. I got this fine freak who likes that nose candy. She already got a hotel room. Man, we going to pull double duty on this little bitch tonight."

"Man, I got these freaks right here."

"Man, leave them tricks alone. I got this, come on. Dude, she is fine as hell, and did you see her body? She got that booty you can set a six pack on."

"Alright, ladies. Roman is leaving you now."

"Why you got to go?"

"I got your number. I'll holler at you later. Man, this shit better be worth it."

"Trust me, it is."

"Candace, baby, you ready?"

"Yeah, I'm good. Let's go."

We got back to my hotel, and that's when my whole world flipped upside down.

Chapter 15

CANDACE

I ended up fucking them both, got high all night and into the next morning. That started my crazy situation with them.

Oh shit, I got to meet their asses. Why in the fuck did I even tell them I was coming to the A? I had no fucking idea they'd follow me. I catch an Uber to the bar.

When I get there they're standing their dumb asses outside. "Hey, Tony, hey, Roman. I'm here, so what the fuck y'all want?"

"Come on, little mama. You want to hit this weed before we go up in here?"

"No, I don't want any of that shit. Let's just go in and get this shit over with. The sooner I can get rid of you both, the faster you'll be out of my life."

I could spit fire; they're pissing me off so bad. My hands are literally shaking, and I have to hold it together so no one can tell I'm in trouble.

"Don't be so mean. Let's go in and grab a drink. We can talk inside."

As always, the music is bumping and I'm not even going to be able to enjoy myself. I do get a chance to talk to my girl, so she can watch my back.

"Hey, sexy. Can I get a crown apple on ice?"

"Yeah, what y'all drinking?"

"Antonio, man, what you want?"

"A corona with a lime."

"Candi, what you want? Let me guess…an apple martini."

"Yes, that's cool."

"Thanks, keep the change. Alright, let's pull up at this table right here. Candi, why does it seem like you've been trying to duck us and shit?"

"Roman, what the fuck are you talking about? I do have a job that I have to go to everyday and make shit happen. Running that fucking money through my club is not easy. I got to sneak. My girls are getting suspicious and shit. I don't know how much longer I'm going to be able to do this."

"Man, calm that shit down. We just here to talk to you to see where we at. Shit, here, man, take this shit and go hit it and calm your ass all the way down."

"No, I don't want any of that shit."

"Yes the fuck you do. Here, girl, go ahead and take this shit 'for I ram it up your nose my damn self."

"Fuck y'all," I say and take the shit. Why can't I say no to this shit? My ass ain't going to be no damn good.

Oh cool one bathroom. I can lock the door without being interrupted. Just got my nails done, so I can slide that shit on my pinkie. I sniff it up one nostril, hit it up the other, and in no time I'm flying high. I go back and sit down with a smile on my face.

Antonio says, "There she goes. You flying, girl, ain't you?"

All I can do is nod.

"Look, fellows, I got this handled. The money's looking good and everything is how it should be. No more talk about that we are in the A. Let's drink and party and enjoy this music."

Roman says, "If you say everything's cool, we're going to trust you. Let's party."

Chapter 16

CANDACE

I miss my flight back to Pittsburgh and I'm going to have to hear Eva's damn mouth.

Shit, let me just give her a damn call and get it out the way. Where is my damn cell? Oh shit, up under my fucking clothes.

"Eva, I got to stay in Atlanta one more day."

"Why, what's the problem? I thought you completed the deal with the new client."

"I did, but it's nice here and I don't get to come here often. I wanted to get some shopping done. Girl, I'll catch a flight out first thing in the A.M.. Shit, Eva, stop being my mama. I'm a grown ass woman who works hard and gets the job done. Why the fuck are you riding me?"

With a sigh, Eva says, "Alright, Candace. Stay out of trouble. See you when you get back."

"Bye, Eva."

Had I known what I know now, I would've got the hell out of there that day.

Antonio and Roman are the local drug dealers from the North Side. They have the Hill and the east side sowed the fuck up. So I thought I hit the jackpot when I met them. My thoughts were, *I am never going to have to buy coke again*. Little did I know that I was going to be paying for it with my life?

They said they had a Columbian connect and that their other boy, Sergio, was bringing it through.

Well, that didn't happen. Sergio somehow got robbed of their shit and got killed. The Columbians didn't want to hear that mess, so now they wanted their money ASAP. 2.5 million in a few weeks, and they wanted triple of what they gave Sergio. They weren't playing around.

Roman and Antonio lost their damn minds. All I wanted to do was get the hell out of there.

But they said I was going to have to run money so they could get this shit back.

"What the fuck you mean, 'run money'? I don't have access to that much money."

"Bitch, you done told us you and those friends of yours have a whole exclusive club that sells pussy all day every day."

"We got some connects out of town. We just don't have a safe way to transport the money for the drugs."

"So that's where you and your club will come in. When you make transfers, you're going to skim from the top, a little of ours and a lot of y'all's."

"We got four weeks, but we got to look at it as if we got three. These motherfuckers from Columbia don't play."

"Man, we got to find out what happened to Sergio and who did that shit and get even."

Roman stated, "Until then we got to get back to Burg and make this shit happen. Them Columbiana's don't fuck around when it comes to their shit."

"They don't know me."

"But we do, and if you don't do as you're told, we'll kill you and them dumb bitches you call friends."

This is my life, and I don't see it getting any better if I don't do something about it quickly.

It's like I'm in a zombie state all day trying to make it seem like everything's all-good when clearly it's not. I'm behind on all my bills, I'm doing coke all day just trying to make it through, and I know the girls can tell something is wrong because I'm not the feisty, energetic, fun loving Candace I used to be. These simple motherfuckers have been in hiding for a while now. They weren't exactly the big time drug dealers they told me they were. They're actually the bottom feeders who are trying to make a big time come up.

Shit, they still don't know what happened to Sergio. It's just a matter of time before the Columbians get a hold of them and take them both out. They think just because it's been months, that they're in the clear. This whole time we been getting this money, or should I say I've been getting this money, for them. We got only one million five. I don't know how or where the other money is going to come from. I'm all dried up. I can't keep running money through the club. They're bound to get suspicious.

It's just best for me to leave for a while and gather my thoughts until I can come up with a solution. I need to try and talk to Mayor Campbell.

I had to get away from these two brothers ASAP, and I couldn't tell the girls where I was going or why I decided to go.

I just have to leave. I don't even have family I can talk to, and I stopped talking to my parents years ago. When my father passed away I vowed never to look back. My siblings never even thought to contact me to see if I was okay, so the hell with them.

I'm on my own. I got myself in it; I got to think of a way to get myself out.

I have a condo up town that no one knows about. I'll just go there and hide out until I figure this shit out.

Chapter 17

DESIREE

The day is going by smoothly. Clients are calling and we have all of our rooms filled. All of a sudden I hear a loud commotion down in the foyer. It sounds like someone busting in the main door.

Frantically, I call down to Frank to see what's happening, but Frank doesn't answer.

I run to the surveillance room to see what's happening.

Damn, that's the couple who came in last month who said they're interested in becoming clients.

Shit! They're actually feds. What the fuck is happening? It seems like they came with the whole damn team. By this time they have the girls and their guests in handcuffs questioning them.

Thank goodness there are no high profile clients here.

I have to call Eva. "Shit, answer your phone. Eva, we have a situation."

"What's going on, Desi? Why you sound so crazy?"

"Girl, we are being raided."

Eva squeaks, "What? That's not possible."

"I'm telling you I'm looking right at it. They haven't found me yet and I don't see Charlotte anywhere. Frank's talking to them right now. This shit got me hot ass mad."

"I thought Mayor Campbell said we'd never have to worry about this type of stuff happening."

There were some important papers on my desk and now I can't seem to find them. "I'm putting a call into him right now. Are you sure they're feds?"

"*Yes,* Eva, they are," Desi growls in frustration. "I'm as sure as the color of my skin they're feds."

That would only mean there's something else going on besides us selling ass. I'm pretty sure it's not about the guns or the drugs. Frederick handles that and he would've said something.

"Well whatever the hell it is," Eva says, "we can't go down like this. Hold on, I got his secretary on the line. Mayor Campbell, please, this is Eva Lavelle. He'll know who I am, this is urgent.

Shortly, the mayor answers, "Eva, what's so urgent?"

"Mayor, right now my place is being raided by the feds."

"Eva, I heard that something was about to go down, but I never would've thought the Feds were watching. Some of my friends at the police department were saying that they heard there's money laundering going on."

"Laundering money who?" Eva scrunches her nose in confusion and anger. "No way in hell! Jason, that's crazy. We're not moving money illegally. We got enough shit we're doing without being as stupid as to launder money through our fucking club!"

Eva yells out loud, trying to release some of her anger. "You don't think that when you heard something like that it would've been a courtesy to bring it to my attention ASAP? I could've got a handle on it right away before it came to this. I suggest you make this shit go away or I'll make your life hell."

"Now wait, Eva, we've been friends for years and I've been helping you with your place all this time. Why in the hell would I risk myself, or you? If I even thought it was a big problem I would've told you."

"Well damn, Jason, this seems to be a *big fucking problem*," Eva screeches into the phone, spit flying everywhere. "The feds are at my establishment. Get to the bottom of this shit."

"Let me see what I can find out." He sounds like he's trying to calm down, but obviously isn't doing well. "They're not going to shut you down or arrest anyone. They're trying to get people to talk, and as long as your people don't open their mouths about anything, you'll be fine. I'll call you in a little while. Just stay low for now and, as soon as I find out anything, I'll contact you."

"Just what in the hell am I going to tell my clients?" she yells.

"Ensure them the problem will be handled and move the workers to the other spot."

"Okay," Eva says with a defeated sigh. "I'll handle it. Talk to you later."

Chapter 18

MAYOR CAMPBELL

This bitch is getting on my last nerve. I got to do something quick before her dumb ass takes all of us down. "Marcy, get Captain Andrew on the phone for me."

"Jason, you have another call on hold for you."

"Who is it?" To himself, he says, "I need to make that other call first." Shaking his head, he says her, "Tell them I have to get back to them later."

"She said it's urgent."

"Well who is it?"

"Her name's Candace."

He rolls his eyes and winces at the pain thumping at his temple. "Put her through right now." *Click.* "Candace, how have you been? I haven't heard from you in a while, what's going on?"

"Jason, I really need to talk to you, but please don't tell Eva or anyone I contacted you."

"Okay, sweetie, I won't. Where are you at?"

"I'll be up town. I'll text you the address. Can you please hurry?"

"I'll be there. I'm leaving here now."

Chapter 19

EVA

"Desi, are you still there?" I'm nervous as hell. Why is this stupid shit happening now when everything is going fine? It's always something to fuck it up.

"Yeah, I heard everything." I'm about to wear a hole through this carpet if I don't stop pacing. "Now why in the hell would they think we were moving money?"

"I don't know, girl. Jason will get the answers we need. In the meantime, let's get everybody moved downtown."

"I'm on it." Where did I put those car service numbers? I think six suv's should work. As soon as these sons of bitches leave I'll inform Frank and the staff."

"We can't shut down completely. We have to maintain some sort of front, so they don't get suspicious."

"We'll work those details out tomorrow. If we close down early today it'll just appear that they shook us up."

"You stay on top of that and I'll call you as soon as I hear back from the mayor."

"Alright, Eva." She pauses. "Please, we got to do something about this sooner than later."

"There's no way I'm letting this situation mess up my money."

"I hear you. Mine either."

We hang up. *Damn, I forgot to tell her who those bastards are.*

Ring! Ring! Ring!

"Hello."

"Eva, girl, do you remember the couple who came in when Sam was visiting?"

"Huh? What are you talking about?"

"It's that damn couple who was talking about hosting parties and becoming clients. She said her husband couldn't get it up anymore."

"Oh Shit!" Them dirty motherfuckers. I'm never off when it comes to fake ass people. "I remember them. They were saying they needed a place to go where maybe her husband could relax and just enjoy watching her have a sexual encounter. She said it was more for her because her husband had a very hard time sustaining an erection."

"Limp dick, my ass. Fuck them! I'll get them dirty bastards back.

"Eva, just calm down. We'll be fine."

"Handle what's going on there and I'll handle Jason."

Chapter 20

EVA

Moving everyone downtown was such a headache. What made matters even worse was the fact that we had to resort to having business parties. For the last three months.

It brings in nice money, but not as much as we usually bring in selling pussy. We have to do what we have to do until some of this shit blows over. We're starting to get some kind of order back when I notice I haven't heard anything from Candace in while.

Has anyone seen Candace? It's been like two months and no word? This is crazy. She disappears like this without saying anything to anyone. She does her disappearing acts, but at least checks in from time to time to let me know she's alright.

Why in the hell does she always do shit like this? Why the fuck is this intercom…Oh, if I press the right key. "Hey, Desi, can you come down to my office please?"

"Yeah, give me a sec; I'm setting up a room arrangement. Why in the hell do you have that depressing ass music on? Never mind, you don't have to answer that."

"Well hold up. I can ask you over the phone."

"Yeah, girl, what is it?"

"Have you heard from Candace? It's not like her not to call or check in."

There's a pause before Desi replies, "As a matter of fact, I haven't heard anything from her. I'll ask the other girls and Frank if they know anything."

"Why the hell does she do this to us? She goes off on her party sprees and forgets she has a job. I don't care if she handles her business when she's not here. That's not the point, it's just unacceptable. If I got to be here, so in the hell does she."

"I agree," Desi says with a sigh. "When she gets back we're going to have a long talk with her about her priorities. If she wants to stay or if she just wants us to buy her out, she can be free and clear to party all the time if she chooses. But this shit right here has to stop. We don't know if she's dead or alive."

"Hey, Desi let me get back at you in a second. I got a call coming in." The line clicks over. "Jason, finally, you decide to call me back? Did you get this handled?"

"Yes, we caught up to the person who started this whole mess. We found out who's been laundering money and, believe me, you're not going to be happy."

"What? Who?"

"Eva, I think you should sit down."

"I'm already sitting just tell me.

"It's Candace."

"Candace?" *Why in the hell would Candy be laundering money?* "You have to be mistaken."

"I wish I was, sweetheart. When we caught up to her she broke down and told us everything. She called me to set up a meeting saying she had something to disclose. I had to make sure what she told me checked out before I came to you. She couldn't handle the pressure on her own anymore. She had nowhere else to turn."

I'm very confused as to what she could've been thinking.

"Listen, Eva. You're going to have to end up letting her go. She's not in a good way, and I don't trust that she won't open her mouth to the feds. She's just not thinking clearly. We need to dispose of her now, before any of this gets out."

"Let me talk to her and see what the hell she was thinking."

"She was very clear that she didn't want to see you or any of the girls. She made me promise not to tell you."

"Fuck that, Jason," I yell. "You need to let me know where she is right now."

"I put her far off the radar in a faraway location, just in case she decided to run."

I don't think she's far enough, if she fucked us up like this. "I need to see her."

"I'll have a car come pick you up in fifteen minutes."

"Thanks, Jason."

"No problem. I'll meet you there."

Chapter 21

EVA

Jason wasn't lying when he said a faraway location. We must have driven for more than an hour. When we arrived it was pitch black, I'm shocked to see that we're far enough in the country no one will find this in a million years. It's secluded. I can't really tell where we are exactly, from it being pitch black. All I know is that there's a lot of dirt, almost like a development of some sort.

I walk in and Candice is sitting there crying and apologizing. The place reeks of mildew. It's dirty and wet like it's stormed for days at a time.

"What are you sorry for, Candy?" *Are you sorry you got caught by the dumb shit you were doing and never thought anyone would find out?* "Why in the hell would you jeopardize what we all worked so hard for? I don't understand. Explain yourself."

"Fuck you, Jason. You promised you wouldn't tell Eva. Why is she here?"

Jason shrugs. "She asked to see you. You girls have been friends for years. She's like your sister, and you should've gone to her before it got this far out of hand."

"I'm sorry, Eva." *Can't you tell I'm miserable? I don't know why I did anything that I did.*

Candace, I don't care that there's snot running down your damn face, or the fact that your eyes are blood shot red. For all I know you're high as fuck right now and will say anything to get you out of this shit.

"I'm so sorry I didn't tell you what I was going through. I just didn't know how. Things just got way out of control. I met up with the wrong people and, once I realized what was happening, I was in over my head and it was too late."

"But why run that shit through our club?"

"It was the only way to make it legit. They threatened to kill me if I didn't do what they said."

"So at that point it didn't dawn on you to come and talk to me? You know damn well that with the connections we have, someone would gladly handle anything for you. All you had to do was tell someone what was happening."

"I stayed so high and out of it I knew you girls wouldn't let me live it down, and I already felt bad enough. How could I say I was jeopardizing our club for two bit thugs? To make matters worse, I think they were playing me."

"How so?"

"They said the Columbians would kill them. See, their boy Sergio had a large package to deliver, but he never made it. Someone killed him at the drop and, seeing that the package was gone, they wanted their money. The guys didn't have all of it, so they had to figure out what to do, and they came up with the idea to move the money illegally. Exchange fake bills for the real money and buy dope. That way they could still salvage some of the lost. In no time they'd have made all the money back and the Columbians would trust them enough to start letting them move product for them again."

"Candace," I say, "What I do not understand is what in the fuck does that have to do with you?"

"I was blowing coke with them when this all went down. They said I'd have to help them get it back or else they'd kill me and you girls."

"Why didn't you tell them you don't have access to that kind of cash?"

"I'd already told them about our club."

"How fucking stupid was that, Candace?" *I knew I should have gotten rid of you a long time ago, but I always wanted you to be close by so we could look out for you.* "You put us all in a fucked up situation. The damn feds have been breathing down our throats for the dumb shit you've been doing."

I go over to her and slap the shit out of her. Her head snaps back, blood trickling down her chin. She loses her balance and falls to the floor. She's never seen that part of me before and I kind of feel sorry for her dumb ass because I know she got caught up with them while she was in party mode. That still doesn't make it right for her to be so damn dumb.

I run up on her and kick her in the gut. She has me so fucking pissed, all I can see at this point is me beating her ass.

"You could've talked to any of us. Now you have us being investigated by the fucking feds."

She grabs her ribs and pleads, "Eva, please. I'll do whatever you want me to do, just stop. I can't die this way. I'll leave town and never show my face around here again."

Unfortunately, baby girl, that's just not good enough for me. "I know you won't show your face around here again, if I have anything to say about it."

"You know we can't have something like this going on. We have too many high profile clients who would be at risk of losing everything. Including us, because your ass was too dumb and had to get involved with some loser ass jack asses."

So I do the only thing I know to do to make sure this shit doesn't come back to haunt me. I already have enough shit to take to my grave, and I just added one more thing to that list.

"Damn, Candace, not you. Out of everyone, I would not have ever thought you'd do anything like this." This is fucked up on all levels. I have to think fast on how to handle this scenario.

"Eva, I'm begging you, please stop!"

"It's time to think fast," Jason says.

I turn to him. "What do you want us to do?"

You have no idea how much this saddens me. "You know what has to be done."

"Eva, nooooooooo," she moans. "Please don't. I'm sorry. I'll make it up to you."

"I'm sorry too, baby girl," I say in resignation. "You know what has to be done. If only you would've come to me, all of this could've been avoided."

"I promise." Her eyes are wild. "Just don't kill me please, Eva!

I watch my friend crying and shaking uncontrollably. She pisses and shits all over herself. Pathetic. I actually feel sorry for her, but it's too late.

"I'll meet you in hell, Eva! Eva! Eva, nooooooooo!"

I walk out and give the signal and, just like that, the house blows up.

BOOM!

The blast is so strong it actually blows me to the ground. I fucking scrape up my knees and hands. Now I'm equally pissed because I just messed up a three thousand dollar Chanel dress.

We can't take any chances. We have to get back to business without any interruptions. Definitely not from the feds or any another law enforcement agency that we don't have on payroll.

I can never speak of this again. It has to be like she never existed. I'm going to miss her and all the fun we shared. At least I know no one will come looking for her. She didn't speak to her family and, if they're still around, they don't know her whereabouts. Damn, Candace, why would you be so stupid?

With the feds off our asses, we can go back to doing what we do best, which is selling sex, drugs, and getting rid of the arsenal we have.

Chapter 22

EVA

Months have passed and it seems like everything is good again.

Everybody gets comfortable back at our regular spot. Pussy Chronicles is again open for business. Their nerves have calmed down about the feds, but now the girls are asking about Candace.

"Hey, Eva," says Charlotte. "Have you heard from Candy?"

Oh shit, here we go.

"No, and I've been trying her for months. I put some calls through, but no word. You haven't heard anything either, huh?"

Desi says, "We haven't heard anything, and that's strange. She never stayed away this long before."

"Well," I say, "You know she was always saying this wasn't forever. She wanted to do her own thing, but not to say anything to her girls."

"Something feels really wrong," Charlotte says softly.

"I'm sure she'll show up. Until then, let's get this place back up and running in the green again."

Suddenly, Desi says, "I'm going shopping. I need to pick up the new Louis Vuitton bag that just came out.

Charlotte says, "Don't you have enough of that man's bags?"

"A girl can never have too many purses."

We laugh and shake our heads.

"Ladies, see you when I return," Desi says. "Are you sure you're going to be good until I get back?"

"Desi, we'll be just fine. I'm going to get ready for our three very important clients who'll be here in second."

"Alright, see you all later."

"Bye, girl."

"Charlotte," I call out. "Can you make sure Queen is ready for her client, please?"

"Yes, ma'am, I surely can. I'm so glad you decided to get these intercoms installed. It makes life so much better. Queen, your client is ready for you. He's in the sun room."

"Okay, I'm on my way, thanks."

Chapter 23

QUEEN

I've always loved this long hallway. It reminds me of something out of Gone with the Wind. Just really classic. It's always very bright and, with the sun coming straight through the skylights, it's beyond pretty.

Queen says, "Jasper, I hope you weren't waiting long."

"No, beautiful, I just got here." A pro basketball player, Jasper stands about 6'5. If you ask him, he'll say he's the shortest one on the team. He has the most beautiful skin you'll ever see. His body's hard, and that man's dick is the size of two thick cucumbers put together.

"How are you?"

"I'm great now that I'm seeing you."

"This is for you. Excuse my shaking hands. You always make me so nervous."

"Aww, a rose! Thank you. That was really sweet of you."

He's sitting on the end of the bed, just a little nervous as he always is, but he's fine, and I'm going to give him something he's never going to forget.

He enjoys the sunroom since it's well lit. He likes to see every detail when we're fucking.

"You ready, Jasper?"

"I'm more than ready." *Just the thought of you gets my dick hard.* "I've been thinking about you for two weeks straight. I couldn't wait until training was over, so I could race back here to see you."

I go to stand in between his legs and push him down on the bed. Slowly, I undo his belt buckle while I kiss and lick his neck.

He's palming my ass like he's holding onto his basketball. "Mmmmm, baby. I like when you squeeze my ass like that."

I slide down his pants with one foot. He grabs my breasts and starts to suck on them. He caresses my nipples, squeezing them like they're the ripest melons he's ever touched.

"Yes, that feels so good. Keep squeezing and sucking them like that. Ahhhhhhhh."

"Queen, you smell so good. That's why I always pick you. You have this incredible scent. It always makes me lose my mind."

He picks me up and wraps my legs around his strong waist. He takes me over by the wall and enters me with a vengeance.

"Yes, fuck me just like that." He's grabbing my hair, licking up my neck, and pumping me faster and faster.

While he's palming my ass, with one swift pull he has my cheeks spread apart just enough so he can stick two fingers in my asshole.

"Mmmmmmmm, Jasper. Oh, baby, you fuck me so damn good. Yes, Yes, Yes."

"Queen, this is going to make me cum," he grunts.

"Yes, cum with me. I want to suck that cum right out of you."

"Here, baby, get on your knees now! Give it to me. Oh, shit, suck this dick. Swallow all of it."

He's hitting the sides of my jaws and I'm taking it. I feel him about to unload down my throat. He grabs my head with both hands and holds his momentum.

"Oh, Queen, Queen, here I cum. Here I cum right now!"

Damn, I have a mouth full of cum. He must have built up from the last time he came and visited me a month ago.

That's funny. I can tell he's been eating pineapples, it so sweet.

"Are you alright? I didn't hurt you, did I, baby?"

"No, I love when you take charge like that."

When you're rough, I know you're enjoying yourself.

"I hate to run off like this, but if I don't make practice or I'm late, coach will have my head."

"It's fine I'll see you next time. Bye for now, Jasper."

Chapter 24

EVA

"Eva, we have a situation."

Can you not come busting in to my office.

"What Frank?" *You sure know how to infuriate me.*

"That shipment that was due to be picked up is being seized right fucking now."

Oh my God, Oh my God. "How did someone even spot it?"

"There's a leak somewhere. I swear, everything was good and going as planned, but as soon as it was to leave, the feds intercepted it."

"That can't be possible. I didn't give Frederick any information about the where's and what's. How the fuck did someone know about that shipment? They confiscated everything?"

"Yes, Eva, we are fucked. We have nothing left, and the Columbians don't even want to deal with us anymore because we didn't secure this shipment. It's too much of a risk."

I'm going to kill that fucking Frederick. We need that supply to get to Texas. "Man, where in the fuck can we come up with that much shit in so little time to send to all the other dealers?"

"Eva, there's no way that anyone is going to touch us right now. We just lost a shit load of money that we can't get back. And, furthermore, we lost the trust of the Columbians. You better be glad we paid them up front or we'd all be dead right now."

With Iron Man not being able to circulate there's going to be a helluva lot of hate that's getting ready to come to us.

"We insured that delivery. Our people were standing by to pick it up and, when it didn't show, they got suspicious. I called in some favors and found out the truth."

Man, why does it seem like shit is falling apart right before our eyes? "I need to speak to Fred and find out if he had anything to do with this. Please hand me my purse out of the chair, so I can grab the burner phone. I don't want to make calls from the landline."

"Judge Frederick Malone, please."

"May I ask who is speaking?"

"Eva Lavelle."

"Hold one second, please." In the background I can hear her call out, "Judge Malone, you have a call on the line one."

"Judge Malone here," comes through the receiver.

"Frederick, how in the fuck could you have stopped my shipment?"

"Eva," he says with a tone less enthusiastic than the one he answered with. "Nice to hear from you as well. What are you talking about?

"I just got word that my product was confiscated by the feds. When speaking with you last, you said you needed that drop to be stopped. The feds are already looking at us for that money laundering shit, we don't need this shit, too."

"Eva, I honestly don't know what you're talking about. I was waiting on you to let me know when it was going to get wherever it was going. When I didn't hear from you, I contacted the attorney general and told him we were going to have to try something different."

"Well, what the hell?" How in the world did they find out about our shit? No one with us would ever say anything. Fuck, we can't lose that like this.

"Let me make some calls and see what I can come up with."

"I appreciate that, Fred."

Chapter 25

DECEPTION

I'm sitting here wondering why I got myself involved in all of this. I took on some things I knew was going to come back and bite me in the ass. My wife, my kids, I can't let them suffer from all the debt I got us into from my gambling addiction. It's about to get my whole family killed if I don't come up with this money as soon as possible. I just pray she never finds out it was me.

I've been working with someone I've never seen, and the only contact has been over the phone by a computerized voice. I know it's all-legit. I just have to get the money I was promised. I need to get this call to put my life back in order.

"It's done."

"Okay good. Your payment will be transferred to your account in less than one hour."

Chapter 26

EVA

I have to stop thinking about Candace. Damn, why did she have to be so stupid? All she had to do was come to me and let me know what was going on. I could have helped her out of anything if she'd not have let it got that bad.

Fuck this shit! I'm not going down for this. *Come on, Eva, we got too much shit to do. Get your head back in the game, girl.* I won't let this consume me, I won't.

Just let me get this paperwork done. I got to get ready for our next client.

Chapter 27

EVA

"Mr. O'Shea," I say with a killer smile, "Your girls are ready for you. Charlotte, can you please take our guest to the oval room."

When I say the oval office, I literally mean oval. The furniture is antique in all the finest woods from around the world. Eva and us girls handpicked everything ourselves, with the help of our interior designer. The paintings are from the 1800 era. It's just a timeless room, and Mr. O'Shea loves this room. When he comes, he always says it reminds him of home growing up as a young boy. So we are always happy to accommodate him.

"Mr. O'Shea, this way. The ladies we have for you are your regular girls Kristi and Becca. We know how you like them, young and very freaky."

He chuckles. "Charlotte, you always make me laugh."

This gentleman is one of our older clients, but don't let that fool you. He's in great shape and very nice looking with his salt and pepper hair.

He totally likes the hands-on approach.

He wants to know what your skin feels like under his touch. He wants to sink his nose in your neck to get the full experience of your smell. If you're touching yourself, he wants to be up close to see exactly what it's doing to you.

"Girls, did you miss me?" *Ladies as rare as you all are is definitely something I've missed.*

"Ol, big daddy, we sure did," Kristi says enthusiastically.

Becca pouts. "What took you so long to come see us?"

"Well, my dears, work keeps me pretty busy. I'm here now, so let's make the best of it."

Kristi says, "Yes, let's get you comfortable."

"You pretty ladies always surprise me with what you can do with your mouth."

"Mr. O'Shea, it's our pleasure to please you. You just lay back and relax." For his age, he sure has a giant size dick that stays very hard; he never needs Viagra to sustain his erection.

Becca takes his penis in her hand and stares up at him as she slides her tongue from the base of his balls to the tip of his dick. He instantly starts growing.

"Becca, that feels great. Suck it, my dear."

"Right there just like that. Come kiss me. Your lips are so soft."

Becca says, "Mr. O'Shea, I'm getting so wet."

"Yes, dear. Come up and let me feel you."

As he sits on the edge of the bed, Kristi comes up between his legs, turns around, and places his dick in her hand. She guides it to her very wet pussy.

He lets out a long sigh, which means he's enjoying what she's doing to him. She's opening and closing her pussy real tight on his dick as she rides him.

He reaches around to squeeze her titties and she gasps.

This older gentleman definitely knows what he's doing.

"Yes, sir. Don't move. Let us do all the work. I feel you getting so very hard."

"That's it, Kristi. You girls are so lovely. I'm so glad you like pleasing an old guy like me."

"Mr. O'Shea, you are far from old."

"My dear girl your mouth is working miracles. Girls, I'm getting ready to cum."

Kristi says, "Oh, oh, oh yes. Cum on me."

"Becca, ride my dick. That's it, let me see that ass shake."

"Yes, you're so hard."

"Becca, I want you to squirt all over me."

"Yes, Mr. O'Shea, here it comes. Are you ready?"

"Yes, my dear. Do it."

"Mmm, here it comes right now."

He looks like he's having a seizure, but I know he's just an older gentleman getting ready to explode from a little too much excitement.

"Splash it all over my mouth." He turns his head and sticks out his tongue, looking like he's trying to catch flies with his mouth. Instead of their piss going in his mouth, it's going all over his face. He just wipes it away and keeps opening and closing his mouth.

"It's like a firehose is coming out your pussy. I'll never understand how you girls do that, but, however you do it, I like it."

"I haven't cum like that in a long time. Since my Lucille left I never thought I'd want another lady or even have the thought of two young ladies that would want to entertain an older gentleman like myself. I sure appreciate my friend who suggested Pussy Chronicles to me."

You have no idea how much this means to me, he thinks, *to be important again to someone, even if it's for only a couple of hours.*

"Now take this extra and go and buy something nice."

Becca says, "Mr. O'Shea, you out-do some of the young guys that we see. You'll have no problem finding another love of your life."

"Oh, my sweet girl, there was only one love of my life, and I know I won't find anything like that. So I'll be content with this."

As long as I can come here and see such beautiful creatures as you all, my life is worth living.

"Thank you, ladies, so much for your time. I must get back. Someone has to run Capitol Hill."

"See you again."

"Don't stay away so long next time."

"We miss you here."

With a chuckle, he says, "I'll definitely be back sooner than later. Have a good evening, until the next time."

Chapter 28

EVA

It takes him a little time to get back to the front area. He likes to stop and look at the cameras on the wall showing what's going on in the rooms. We have them in the part of the house that only our special guests know about. It's certainly not for random clients. You have to be VIP to get in that area.

Eva says, "Mr. O'Shea was everything to your liking?"

"Yes, they are very much to my liking. It just brings me joy to know that two beautiful ladies don't mind pleasing an old man like me."

"I'm so glad you enjoyed yourself. Will you be coming back sometime soon?"

"As I stated to the two beautiful young ladies, it will be sooner than later."

"That's just fine. Hector will summon your driver. Have a safe flight back to Washington, sir."

"Thank you, Eva. You have a great evening."

"I plan on it."

It's always good to see a high profile client leaving with a smile on his face.

That was the last client for today. Now I need to get home before the traffic gets bad.

"Frank, I'll see you and the girls back here tomorrow. Have a good night."

Damn, it was raining. Waiting for valet seems like it takes forever, but, finally, there's my car.

"Thank you, Hector." I hand him a hundred dollar bill.

"Thank you, Ms. Lavelle."

"No problem, Hector. Can you please get my door before I get soaked out here?"

"Yes, Ma'am. You have a good evening."

"I'm sure going to try."

Traffic is heavy, but I finally make it home. I run and take off my clothes at the front door.

I start my bath and pour me a glass of my favorite red wine, which is a great Merlot. After lighting my candles, I add rose petals to my bath with almond milk. Then I play my Pandora.

Sade, she always puts me in the right mood when I need to get lost within myself.

Thinking about Candace and knowing that she's dead is becoming a bit much for me to take. It overwhelms my daily thoughts. I can't eat, I'm not sleeping properly, and all I do when I try to sleep is toss and turn. I'm being haunted with images of Candace.

The screams coming from her while she was burning and I literally just let her die. I couldn't let what she did fuck up what we worked so hard for. I knew Candace was young when we started Pussy Chronicles, but she was very smart and had a great mind for business. She promised she wouldn't let her partying ways interfere with our company.

Everything started off great. It wasn't until later that her life got in the way of her success. The drugs started to become first in her life. It was always so easy for her to get access to them. She'd say that it wasn't something she'd do every day. It was a weekend party thing. The girls and I saw something very different happening. We knew Candace was struggling with the fact that her mother wasn't speaking to her, and her siblings followed suit with whatever their mom felt.

Candace knew she had family with us, it just wasn't enough. I knew when she got with those no good hustlers it was going to be a problem. Oh God, what have I done? How did I allow myself to get so caught up in this mess? If I could take it all back, I promise I would.

If anyone finds out that I had anything to do with her death it won't be good.

The girls are asking questions every day. Candace, how you could've been so stupid is beyond me. Damn, girl, I feel so bad about how things worked out, and not for the good. I couldn't take that chance of you getting us caught up in all of your bullshit when I worked so hard to keep this business off the radar. Do you really think I was going to let you fuck this up for all of us? Hell no, Candace. It's your fault that you're dead. You should've thought instead of getting yourself caught up with the wrong damn crowd.

I reach up and grab my glass dildo. The last time I used this was when Samantha was in town. I need her here now, to make me feel good with her tongue. The way she knows how to work it is miraculous. I should just call Michael. He can also put out this fire and clear my mind for a little while. Except he's still upset with me about going out with the girls and not letting him know until the next day. Hopefully, I can make myself feel better even if it's just for a little while.

I sip my wine, sing along with Sade, and dance in front of my mirror. Before I know it, I'm on my third glass. I step into the tub and it feels so good. I begin touching my breasts and squeezing my nipples, bringing my hands up to my neck to feel the softness of my skin.

My hand travels down my stomach and I start massaging my clit. I lift my leg and throw it over the tub, reaching for my dildo. I scoot down just a little and insert my toy.

"Yessssss, this feels so good. Ahhhhhhhh, Ahhhhhhhhhhh, Ahhhhhhhh." I start off slow and then go a bit faster. I take my other hand to pay close attention to my nipples.

"Oh shit." By this time, I'm ramming my pussy something good, and I'm about to bring myself to one of my best orgasms. "Ahhhhhhhhhhhh yessssssss. Oh shit. I'm cumming."

I have to slow my heart down; it is like I just had a very good work out. Jeesh, I really needed that.

I wash up, put my smell good lotion on, and sleep naked. It's the first time in a long time that I'm able to sleep without Candace consuming my dreams. She played a major part in our day to day, and she's no longer here. I took that option from her. I didn't even give her a chance to make amends.

Let me just be thankful that I'm able to get a good night's rest. I'm thankful for that.

When I wake in the morning, something seems a bit off. It doesn't feel quite right, but I can't figure out why I feel like that.

So I try to forget about it. I go to get dressed. It's already noon and I have some errands to run. I want to get to work before three. I have some paperwork to get done.

Chapter 29

EVA

I run to the cleaners to grab my skirt suits, and go past the grocery store to get some items we're out of.

Making it to the Chronicles by 2:30, I notice that the place is quiet, and it's never this quiet. I search for the girls and Frank, only to find them in my office with one of the federal agents who was giving us problems earlier this year.

"Hey, guys, what's going on?"

For some reason my office looks and feels so bleak and dull with everybody just standing around looking at me like they just seen a ghost

"Eva," Desi says, "they found Candace dead."

"What?" I'm about to pass out. I have to keep it together, so it won't show on my face that I'm guilty as hell. "What do you mean she's dead? That can't be possible."

"Ms. Lavelle," Agent Timber says. "When was the last time you saw your business associate?"

"Let's get one thing straight," I say. "She was not just a business associate. Candace is family. We all are. Where did you find her?"

"That's confidential, ma'am. We have to conclude our investigation before we can release any information."

"Oh my God! Why is this happening?" I'm losing it on the inside; it's just a matter of time.

"Ma'am, we'll get to the bottom of this, but in the meantime it would help if you can try and pinpoint the last time you saw her."

"I really don't know. It's been damn near a year. We just thought she wanted out."

The Agent's very confused. "Wanted out from what, ma'am?"

"Um," I swallow. "Her life here at the Chronicles She always talked about moving to a faraway island and starting a family."

"Did any of you try to contact her family?"

"We didn't know anything about her life," Charlotte says. "She never wanted to talk about it"

"She mentioned her parents. Her father passed away some years ago, and her mother and siblings are still alive. But she never wanted to talk about that part of her life. We asked, but she'd say she cut them off a long time ago and there wasn't no going back."

"You all didn't find that odd that she didn't want to have anything to do with her family?"

"Not to be rude, sir, but there are families that don't want to fuck with their family, and we just respected what she said and never asked her again. Besides, Candace was young. We always thought that maybe one day someone would come looking for her, or she'd miss her family and want to reach out. No one ever came and she never went back."

"Can we please have her body, so we can give her a proper burial?" Desi asks.

"Ma'am, there was nothing left."

Everyone just hollers and screams.

"We identified her from dental records. By the time we got there the fire was out of control. We did find two more bodies."

"What did you say?" Two other bodies. What are you talking about?

"Yes we found two males," Agent Timber says. "Once we were able to run DNA, it came back that they're some of the local thugs from the Northside area. Roman and Antonio. Do you happen to have any idea who they might be and why they'd be where we found your friend?"

"Agent," Frank asks, "I didn't catch your name."

"I'm sorry about that. I am Agent Timber, and this is my partner Agent McMillian."

"Agent Timber, I don't mean to be rude again, but how the hell would we know who those two guys are or even know how they're affiliated with Candace?"

"I apologize, ma'am. We have to ask these questions, so we can find out exactly what happened. If you can think of anything else that would help this case, please don't hesitate to give us a call."

"Ma'am," Agent McMillian says, "I was noticing your earring on the desk?"

"Yes, my grandmother gave them to me before she passed."

"They're very lovely. My mother had beautiful antique jewelry like that. It seems you're missing one?"

I lose everything. "I seem to have misplaced it."

"Well, it's a beautiful piece. It'd be such a shame not to find the other one."

I'm hoping it shows up as well. It's the only real item I have from my grandmother.

"Have a good day, everyone," Agent Timber says. "If you need anything else, or have any other questions that we can answer, here is my card. My cell is on the back. Please feel free."

How can they be so heartless? "Charlotte and Desi," I say, "I need you to call Pastor Troy and arrange a service."

"Eva, how could this have happened?" Charlotte asks.

"I don't know, but I'll get to the bottom of this. I'm not going to let her death go unanswered. Someone knows something."

"This can't be happening," Desi says. "We'll never see Candace again. She was only twenty-six. Who'd want to hurt her?"

"I hate to say this, but you know she always partied around people who didn't mean her any good. And it didn't help that she liked to use cocaine on occasion. You know whenever she was flying she thought she was invincible."

"That still doesn't give anyone the right to kill her," Frank says.

"Ladies, I need for you to pull yourselves together. We're not going to get anywhere if we fall apart."

"You're right," Charlotte says. "Candace wouldn't want that, she just wouldn't."

"It's going to be hard, but we will get through this with all our help."

Desi looks at me and asks, "What do you need us to do, Eva?"

"Nothing right now. I need to handle something. Just get in contact with Pastor Troy. Frank, please bring the car around. I need to see Mayor Campbell now."

"Eva, what's wrong?" Desi asks.

"Nothing. I just need to go and see if he can find out what happened to our girl."

"Now wipe your tears, both of you. We'll get to the bottom of this." Desi and Charlotte can never find out or even be involved. They have their families, and I can't let anything happen to them or their families. I couldn't live with that.

Chapter 30

EVA

As I drive to see Jason, I'm losing it on the inside. Roman and Antonio were found dead. How? They weren't there! This has to be some kind of a setup. What the hell have I done? What have I gotten myself into? This shit is getting crazier and crazier. If only I could figure this out, all of this would not be happening. Oh, Lord, what if this is a joke for all that I've done, with all the secrets I have to take to the grave? Is this punishment for that? I didn't have to have her killed.

Antonio and Roman, though, I had nothing to do with. I won't go down for them. Oh, God, what have I done?

Tears stream down my face. I can't keep my hands from shaking. My mind's racing a thousand miles a minute and I can't turn back from this one.

I can't even see where I'm going. Dear God, please don't let me crash. Thank goodness there is a spot right in front of his office.

"Please excuse my face. Where is your restroom, so I can clean up a little bit?"

"Is everything alright right, ma'am?"

"It will be. Your restrooms, please?"

"Oh, I'm sorry. Straight through those glass doors."

"Thank you"

"You're very welcome"

Shit, look at my face. My eyeliner got me looking like a damn fool, running all down my face. There is no way I can clean all this up. Let me just put some cold water on my face.

Lord, I'm probably praying to the wrong person, but I just don't know what I'm doing any more. If you could just please take my hand and guide me where you want me to go, I promise to make things right. Okay, get yourself together and get out there.

"Everything better now?"

"Yes. Mayor Campbell, please. Eva here to see him."

"Wait one minute please."

Look at him, looking like he got his life together.

"Eva, my sweet girl. What brings you by today?"

"Jason, the feds were back at my place. They found Candace's body, but they also found the bodies of Roman and Antonio alongside her."

"How could they have been out there? Did you have them put there?"

"No!" I shout. "Did you?"

"Eva, I don't know anything about those boys. I don't even know them."

"Something is going on," I say. "Someone had to be there and was able to dump those other bodies."

"Who could've seen anything? We were way out in Timbuktu. That fire would've been put out long before anyone would've noticed. Somebody's fucking with us."

"But who, Jason?"

"I don't know, Eva. Candace should've never been found. She was burned and buried alive."

I can't, and I won't, lose everything I worked so hard for. My wife... my kids. I put everything on the line to make this shit go away, he thought to himself.

"Jason, God damn it, they found her teeth along with those fucking thugs! If they connect the dots, we're going down for three murders. We can't have this. Shit, what is happening?"

"How in the hell did they even know to look for her out there? That place is so far off the map, it's impossible."

"Well, damn it, they found her and them. They said they couldn't tell us anything because they're still investigating. If I go down, we both go down. FIX THIS, JASON! We need to find out who's talking or out to get us. Someone knows exactly what we've done, and they're fucking with us."

I can't go to jail behind this bullshit. I snatch up my purse and got the hell out of there like my life depended on it.

Shit, it does depend on it.

Chapter 31

AGENT TIMBER

"Cunningham," I call out. "Come in my office for a second. We need some peace and quiet. There's a lot of shit going on in here today with that big drug bust we just had. Just move that stuff off my chair and sit there."

I know whenever I get some time I'll clean this dusty ass office up. I was doing some thinking about this case and there are somethings that just aren't adding up.

"Marsha, did you notice the earring on Eva's desk?"

"Yes. It's the same earring at the scene."

"Now how would that have been possible if she wasn't there?"

I highly doubt that Candace would borrow one earring. Those are antique's given to her by her grandmother. She wouldn't have loaned them to no one. They're too much of a sentiment to her.

"Get forensics back out there and comb the area fully. We have to find out what exactly happened to those people. Tell them to find anything and everything. Put a rush on it."

Something doesn't smell quite right about this. We need to close the lid on this one before it gets out of hand and we don't ever find out what happened to that young lady or them fucking thugs.

Chapter 32

EVA

It's back to business as usual. We had a small service for Candace. Everything turned out perfect. She had a beautiful service with about two hundred people who showed up for our girl. Her casket was all white. She loved lilies, so we have them all around the room.

Desi picked a portrait of her that I know she would've approved of. She was a beauty. It's just a shame she didn't know how to handle her business. It seems like everything's getting back to normal. Or so I thought.

"Federal Agent Malone, how can we help you?"

"Agent Timber says, "We're here to see Eva Lavelle.""

Desi says, "Is everything alright? Follow me, she should be in her office."

"Eva, Special Agent Timber is here for you."

What is he doing here again? I knew this day would come. I'm so glad I prepared for what's about to happen. My attorneys know exactly what to do if this ever happened.

"Ma'am, you're under arrest for the murder of Candace Sheldon, Antonio Jackson, and Roman Chase."

"What?" I ask in confusion. Then what he says dawns on me. "Wait a minute; I had nothing to do with them. You can't take me to jail. I'll have my attorney's all over your asses before the end of the day."

Obviously not in the mood to drag this out, Agent Timbers holds out a pair of handcuffs toward me. "Will you please just come with us, ma'am?"

Charlotte whispers, "Eva what's happening?" There is a pause, and then awareness sets in. "Did you kill Candace?"

"Why, Eva? So you're just not going to say anything? How the fuck could you just stand there silent? I want to know what the hell is going on."

"Eva, answer us!"

"Did you kill Candace?"

"Everything will be fine, ladies. Get my attorney ASAP. This is a mistake. I would never do anything like this. What evidence do you have against me? This should be real good for you to come barging into my office and accusing me of a crime I did not commit."

I could feel my veins coming through my skin because I was screaming at the top of my lungs. Someone was going to tell me something. I knew I was guilty as hell, but they were going to have to come for me with everything they had.

"So, Agent Timber," I say, a little too haughtily. "I will ask you again what the fuck you think you have on me."

"The day we were here Agent McMillan asked you about your earring. You said you misplaced the other one. That's the same earring we found at the crime scene. I found that quite unusual. If it were an heirloom how could you be so careless with such an item. That made me and my partner dig a little bit further into this investigation."

"That can't be possible! She could've borrowed that earring."

"That was a thought as well," he says with a nod, "but forensics turned up some other evidence. The shoes you were wearing that day also matched the prints left. We gathered your items out of your condo.

"You had no right going to my place without a warrant."

"Ma'am, calm down. We had a search warrant. Your doorman let us in. At the time, you weren't a suspect until we gathered all of the evidence. And wouldn't you know it, the shoes we found in a garbage bag buried in your closet had all the evidence we needed. The mud's a perfect match. Take her in now."

The other Agent says, "We never would've found your friend or those boys had someone from the road above not smelled all the smoke. They decided to call the police."

"Eva, how could you?"

My heart was coming through my chest. I was surely going to pass out any moment.

"I didn't kill those boys. I swear to you I didn't. I don't even know how they got there. Someone is setting me up."

Desi asks, "Eva, did you kill Candace?"

"Ma'am, I suggest you don't say anything else until your lawyer is present. You have the right to remain silent. Anything you say can be used against you in the court of law. You have the right to consult with an attorney and have that attorney present during any questioning. If you cannot afford an attorney, one will be provided for you. Do you understand these rights?"

"Yes."

"With these rights in mind, do you wish to speak with me?"

"Yes, you sons of bitches, I do." I turn to the girls, pleadingly. "It was something you wouldn't have understood. I'm sorry. I'm so, so sorry. We worked so hard for what we have and I couldn't let anyone, including Candace, mess that up for us."

The room is spinning. I think I'm going to pass out. The one place in this mansion, my office, used to be my refuge, but now it seems like a dark place that I don't want to be a part of anymore.

Desi screams. "You bitch! She was just a kid. No, let me at her. Frank, get the fuck off me. I could fuck you up. You know she didn't have family. We were the only family she had, and you killed her for what? Your stupid ass greed I always knew you were trifling but I never thought you could go this far. You know what? Whatever happens to you still won't be enough for killing Candace. I hope they fry your trifling, dirty ass. Go to hell, Eva!"

"Get her out of here before we have another homicide on our hands."

The whole scene, as they take me, is like something out of a movie. There are police cars everywhere, and the news stations are already lining up taking pictures. I break the heel on my brand new pair of Giuseppe Zanotti shoes. Damn, my day just went to pure hell.

I'm arrested for Candace's murder and get life without the possibility of parole. How did I let things get so out of control? Desi, Charlotte, and Sam didn't have anything to do with what I did and I make sure the prosecution knows exactly that it was all me.

Mayor Campbell was off the hook as well. He shot his self in the head in his office late one night. The possibility of getting caught was never in his game plan, so instead of going to jail and making his family look horrible he decided to take his life.

Chapter 33

SAMANTHA

That bitch finally got what she deserves. My greed takes over at this point. Why should I let Eva have all the power? She got the game fucked up if she thinks I'm going to continue to be her flunky and sex slave. All she had to do was make us exclusive and let me have ownership of the Chronicles in the Riviera. I run it all; I just don't have ownership rights. I wasn't getting the money I should've gotten. She thought what I was making was enough when she was making three times more doing the same exact thing.

The city officials, the ballers, the high profile clients, getting those fake ass hustlers killed, and confiscating one of the biggest drug bust of the fucking century—it was all me. If the feds didn't get her, the Columbians would've killed her trifling ass anyway. But that bitch wanted to take credit for everything. She may have started it, but it will be me who finishes it.

I only put up with all that sex and drama to make sure it would all crumble in her fucking face. It was always, "Samantha, make sure you're doing what needs to be done on your end", "Samantha, let me dive into your pussy", "Samantha" this, "Samantha" that.

She was good with her mouth, but I was just as good with my mind. The more I let her dive in this good pussy the more I knew she was getting caught up. I made it a point to book clients in the U.S., so I could make sure my plan took effect.

I'm the one who made sure Candace hooked up with those no good thugs. I knew she liked to powder her nose on occasion. She had no idea I was behind it all, that's how bad I was. This is going to belong to me.

Candace's problem was she was young and liked to party, so I knew Antonio and Roman would be perfect for what I had in mind. She came into this game a little too early to be able to experience all that she was surrounded with. You don't give a young girl power like that and expect her to do exactly what she needs to do to be successful in this game of pussy and deceit. I know all their weaknesses. She'll never suspect that I'm behind the whole fuckery of her demise. Setting her dumb ass up was like taking candy from a baby. Now I can run this company like it should've been ran in the first place.

Chronicles of Deception:

Never trust a pussy with an agenda.

Chronicles of

Deception

THE SAGA CONTINUES

LOVE & LUST EROTIC TALES IS NOW AVAILABLE!

Sex in the City

"Jameson, aren't we going into the city this weekend?" I asked.

"Baby girl, don't I always surprise you with something spectacular on our anniversary?"

"Yes, baby, you do. I just want to make sure the surprise I have for you will be the right flavor." I replied

Confused, Jameson replied, "The right flavor? What does me taking you away have to do with the right flavor?"

"You'll see. It's going to be awesome, and you are going to definitely enjoy yourself."

Needing to make sure we were going where I thought, I asked, "Are we staying at our place in Manhattan?"

"Yes, and that's all I'm going to tell you, woman."

"No more questions, I promise." Kissing him on the lips, I say, "Okay, I'll see you later. I have something I have to take care of."

"Okay, baby. Be careful."

If he only knew my plans for him involved a very beautiful, Hispanic chica by the name of Gabriela.

*****

I met Gabriela at the bar a couple of weeks ago. When I noticed her, I couldn't believe how sexy she was. She was absolutely stunning.

She stood about 5'7", with beautiful, light brown eyes, long, wavy hair, caramel colored skin, and her breasts…my goodness. I could have just started sucking on them right there.

She was wearing a short skirt, although not super short, it was just enough to show off her beautiful, long, legs. She also had on a sequined blouse with a deep plunging neckline, and a long arrow necklace that fell perfectly between her voluptuous breasts.

She was sitting there, alone, so I went up to her and asked her to dance. Shockingly, she said yes. So there we were on the dance floor and I'm practically screaming because the music was so loud.

"Hi, my name is Meghan." I shouted.

"Hola, my name is Gabriela."

Smiling, I told her, "I just wanted to tell you, you are stunning."

"Gracias, Meghan. I think you are beautiful too."

As we continued to grind upon one another on the dance floor, Gabriela said, "Meghan, I hope you don't mind that I am dancing with you like this, but you are so freaking caliente."

"I'm sorry, my Spanish is not good...what does that mean?" I asked.

"It means I think you are hot...sexy."

Blushing I replied, "Thank you."

My pussy was soaking wet just from the proximity of her. She was not only beautiful, but she smelled amazing.

"You are doing things to my insides that only my man has done to me."

We were dancing and feeling up on each other. As we were grinding our pussy's on one another, she whispered in my ear, "¿Te gustaría ir a la sala de estar conmigo?"

"I don't understand what you are saying."

Chuckling she said, "Would you like to go to the ladies room with me?"

"Yes, I would." I answered without hesitation.

"Vamonos!"

I shrugged my shoulders.

Taking her index finger, she gestured for me to follow. Stepping forward, I was right on her heels.

Grabbing my hand, she led me to the restroom. Once we were inside she reached behind her and locked the door.

"Meghan, yo querer a comer tu el hijo de puta."

"I don't understand." I breathlessly answered.

"Let me just show you." she said.

Pulling me toward the sink she gently pats the counter, letting me know to get on top of it. Carefully climbing on top of the counter, I casually hiked my skirt up my legs. Stepping in front of me, she placed her hands on my thighs and gently spread my legs apart. Stepping back for a moment, she admired the view. I was soaking wet.

Bending down in front of me, she carefully pulled my panties aside before sticking her face between my legs. Finding my clit immediately, she began licking, sucking and nibbling.

"Ah, Gabriela, that feels so good." I moaned.

Placing my hand on the back of her head, I gently rocked my pussy on her face. No matter which way I grinded my hips, she kept my clit right on her tongue. Reaching up, she roughly squeezed my breasts before suddenly pinching my nipples between her fingers.

Throwing my head back, I exhaled deeply. This feeling that she was giving me was purely sensational.

I was so lost in the intense feelings I was having that I didn't even notice her hand migrating toward my pussy until I felt her place her long fingers inside me.

"Meghan, use your pussy...squeeze my fingers and don't stop."

"Oh Gabriela, oooohhhh, I'm about to cum. Shit, that's right; suck my clit, keep finger fucking me." I moaned.

"Querer probar tu semen." *Translation: I want to taste your cum.*

I don't know what she said but I was cummmmming down her throat and she was drinking every last drop and loving it.

My legs were shaking and I had sweat running down my face. She had taken my breath away. *She certainly knew exactly what to do with her tongue.*

After regaining my strength, I jumped down from the counter, grabbed her by the shoulders and turned her ass around. I wanted to see that ass from the back. *Damn, she has a pretty ass.*

Bending down, I took my tongue and licked up and down her ass cheek. Placing my hand in the center of her back, I gently pushed down, letting her know to bend over.

"Spread your ass cheeks for me, I want to eat that pussy from the back." I demanded

Diving in between her luscious cheeks I went straight for my prize. *She is so fucking sweet.* Taking my tongue, I would lick up her slit before making my way back down, making sure my tongue grazed her asshole. Continuing to lick, suck and gently nibble, I heard her cry out, "Oh, Meghan, that's so good. Eat me; let me hear you suck on my pussy. That's it."

She took her leg and threw it over my shoulder; she put both of her hands on the back of my head and grinded that pussy all over my mouth.

I was so fucking turned on. This wasn't the first time I had ever had a pretty pussy in my face, but it was the first time I had a pretty Latina pussy in my face; and it certainly wouldn't be the last.

After removing her hands from the back of my hand, she proceeded to pull out her big, beautiful titties. I immediately took each of them big ass titties in my mouth and began sucking and biting each nipple.

"Oh yes, Meghan, suck my titties." she moaned.

Spinning her around I placed her leg on top of the counter before slowly reaching down and rubbing her clit. She was moaning and speaking in Spanish and whatever the fuck she was saying was sounding so good and making my love canal drip.

I reached down and found her clit and started rubbing it. She was moaning and speaking in Spanish, and whatever she was saying it was sounding so good and making my love canal drip.

Taking my hand she forced my finger inside her soaking wet pussy and she kept pushing them further and further inside of her. The further my fingers progressed inside her canal, the more I could feel her clenching my fingers with her pussy. I could tell she was about to cum.

That shit was something fucking different...in a good, nasty way.

"Oh, oh, oh, Meghan, I'm cummmmming. I'm cumming, chica." she moaned.

Pulling me up toward her, she buried her tongue in my mouth and started sucking it. I still had my fingers in her pussy, and I could feel her cumming all over my hand. She continued grinding on my fingers while moaning in my mouth and sensually sucking on my tongue.

Breaking the kiss, she said, "Don't stop, don't stop, Meghan."

I had no intentions on stopping until she was completely finished cumming.

"Oh, Meghan, Si, si, chica. I cannot stop cumming. Oh my, you are so good. Si, si, siiiiii." she shouted.

"Oh my goodness, that took me on such a natural high." I said breathlessly. After catching my breath, I said, "Damn, Gabriela, that was good, girl!"

"Si, Meghan, that was so exhilarating. Please tell me we can get together again real soon?"

"We most definitely will be." *Sooner than you think.* I thought.

After exchanging numbers and promising one another that would talk later in the day, we each left the club and headed home.

*****

This is where my plan came alive. I knew my man was going to surprise me with that 'out of town' trip for our anniversary. *That will be the perfect time to introduce Gabriela to Jameson.*

Jameson and I had been talking about it for several months now, what he didn't know was that I had a treat in store for him. Occasionally, I would sometimes bring him treats, but this treat he was going to devour, and I wanted to see that.

*****

Picking up my cell to Gabriela, I dialed her number. I couldn't help but notice how excited I was to speak with her.

RING. RING.

"Hola." she answered on the third ring.

"Hey, girl! How are you doing today?" I asked.

"I'm good, chica. I'm glad you decided to call. What is good with you?"

"So, Gabby, I wanted to ask you something. Is it okay that I call you that?"

"Si, that is fine. What is it you needed to ask?" she asked sounding concerned.

"My man is taking me out of town for the weekend, for our anniversary, and I was wondering if you would be down to going with us? All expenses will be on us and you will have the time of your life."

"Chica, I'm not like some prostitute or something." she replied, almost sounding offended.

"No, girl, I didn't mean it like that, I promise. It's just that we had such a great time together I just wanted my man to experience what you got between them thighs. You down with that?"

"Oh! Okay, that sounds good; I can do that. Besides, I need a little vacation anyway. Just let me know where and when."

"Cool, I'll call you later so we can make the arrangements."

"Okay, chica, talk to you later. Adios."

*****

After speaking a few more times, ironing out exactly how we were going to play this, I ended up sending Gabriela to our Manhattan spot so she could be ready for our arrival.

I knew we would be going to dinner and a play, so she would have plenty of time to see New York, shop for something sexy and still make it back to our place in time to set the mood.

*****

"Jameson, I love you so much. Thank you for always coming through for me on our special day." I said sincerely.

"Baby girl, all I do is for you and for us. I'm glad you enjoyed your evening and your gifts."

"I got something for you too, baby."

Curiosity lit his face. "What is it?" he asked.

"You'll see later, but right now...I got you." I said with a wicked grin.

Looking around the room, I saw no one was paying us much attention, so I slipped underneath the table."

Startled, Jameson asks, "Meghan, what are you doing?"

"Shhhhhhhh, just relax and enjoy." I whispered.

"Girl, you crazy."

Once I was under the table, I carefully unzipped my man's pants and gently took his dick in my hands. I began slowly stroking him up and down. Just as he was getting used to the feeling I opened my saliva-filled mouth and forced him to the back of my throat. As soon as I got his dick in my mouth his fist banged on the table.

The waiter walked over and asked, "Sir, I'm sorry, did you need another bottle of wine or are you ready for the check?"

"No, I'm fine. I'm just waiting for my wife to come back from the restroom. Shit, that feels good." he answered.

"Excuse me, sir?" the confused waiter replied.

"No, I'm sorry…I was just thinking out loud."

"Okay, let me know if you need anything. I'll be right over there." he said pointing toward the waiter's station.

"Alright, I'll let you know." he said. Once the waiter was out of earshot, Jameson whispered, "Meghan, you got to stop."

"Do you really want me to stop?" I asked before shoving his cock down the back of my throat.

"Nnnnnooo." he stammered. "I don't, but if you don't, this whole damn restaurant is going to know that I'm getting a blowjob under the table."

"Okay, baby, let's take this home and I'll finish there."

Peeking out from under the tablecloth, I made sure no one was watching. Crawling out from underneath the table, I sat in my chair and laughed at his obvious struggle.

Jameson immediately called over the waiter for the check. Once we paid the bill we headed home. On our way home I texted Gabriela so that I knew she was in the guest room waiting for the right time to come out.

*****

"Honey, why don't you go ahead and get comfortable and I'll be back after I freshen up."

"Go ahead, baby. Do your thang, I'll be right here when you get finished."

I headed toward the guest room to tell Gabby we were back. I must have startled her when I walked in. I had to put my hand over her mouth to muffle her voice.

"Damn, you look so good." I whispered in her ear.

Shit, I want to eat her pussy right here, but I'll wait. Kissing her, I told her, "As soon as you see the light go out, come on out."

"Okay." she replied.

I hurriedly put my sexy chemise on, dabbed some perfume in all the right spots and headed back out to my man. *This is going to be a fun fucking night.*

"Baby, are you ready for me?" I asked.

Jameson sat up on the bed. Relaxing on his elbows he replied, "Damn, girl, you are fucking bad."

"Thank you, sweets." I replied sweetly.

As I stood in front of him he just stared at my body before saying, "Come here so I can take that off of you."

"Yes, daddy, take it off."

Staring at this sexy man in front of me, I was so wet just knowing what was about to go down. Jameson was nothing to play with; he is a 6'2", 220-pound strong black brother, with mocha complexion, and lean everywhere. And his dick...his dick is a full nine and a half inches and all mine; though I don't mind sharing occasionally.

Taking off my clothes, Jameson says, "Damn girl, finish doing what you were doing to me in the restaurant."

"What's that, baby? I want to hear you say it."

"Sucking my dick."

"Ah, yes, let me get that."

Sliding down his body, I put him in my mouth sucking him all the way down, back up and around, making my spit drip all down his balls.

"Girl, your mouth be so right."

"Yes, daddy, give it to me. Fuck my mouth."

"Mmmmmmm, Mmmmmmmmmm." he moaned. "Come here, girl, I want to hit it from the back. Bring me that ass."

It's almost time.

As soon as he put his dick in me and I got all into it, I hit that light switch. With the lights out you could still see because it illuminated just enough to see what you needed to see.

Looking back, I could see Gabriela walking towards us, making my pussy get extra juicy. As she tipped-toed toward the bed I started thrusting back real hard on his dick, that way he wouldn't feel her get on the bed.

As soon as I saw her tongue come out of her mouth I had to make sure I held onto his hands. I knew it would startle him and I didn't want him to accidentally punch her.

She gently slid her tongue up his back. He jumped. Turning around he said, "Damn, where did you come from?"

"Surprise, daddy! She is your surprise." I said excitedly.

"Damn, Meghan, she scared the shit out of me." he said breathlessly. "Hold on, let me get my composure back."

After taking a few deep breaths, he said, "Okay, I'm cool." Taking a good long look at Gabriela, he finally said, "Fuck you fine as hell." Turning toward me he said, "I'll ask you how you set this up later, but right now I want to see y'all fuck."

"No, daddy, I want to see you fuck her."

Looking toward Gabriela, I said, "Gabriela this is Jameson."

"Hola, Jameson, I hope you are happy for your surprise."

"Hell yea." he said without hesitation.

"I'm going to watch you fuck her." I said.

James slapped his hands together in preparation of what was to come. Before he knew what hit him, Gabriela had pushed him down on the bed and did what she does best. She was sucking his cock in a fever and Jameson was loving it.

"Oh damn! Oh damn! Shit, girl, your head game is nice," he moaned.

I was so wet watching her suck Jameson's dick. As I watched, I was pulling on my clit and sticking my fingers in my juicy box. You could actually hear how wet I was.

"Yes, Gabriela, suck his dick." I told her.

Glancing over at me finger fucking myself, Jameson said, "Baby, that looks so good."

"Shit, it is good. Lay her down, baby. I want you to fuck that pussy. It's so sweet, taste it."

Lying on her back, Gabby spread them pretty legs for him. Gently, he pulled her pussy apart and licked all over that clit.

"Oh, James, si that feels soooooooooo good. Do not stop sucking my pussy. Meghan, come over here and put your titties in my mouth."

I was certainly happy to oblige. Stepping in front of Gabriela, I placed my titties near her face. Without hesitation, she immediately began sucking and licking on each of my nipples.

"Si, Si, give it to me! Chica, your husband is good with his mouth. Mmmm, your titties taste so good." she moaned.

"Yes, Gabby, suck them and bite them."

"Come put your pussy on my mouth while James fucks me." Gabriela begged.

I slowly eased down upon her face. Damn, she can eat some pussy.

Grabbing my ass, she held me in place. My pussy was so wet I was dripping down her chin.

While Gabriela continued eating my pussy, Jameson put a couple of pillows underneath her ass and rammed his dick deep inside her pussy.

"Oh my God, you are big." she shouted.

Bending down between her legs, I began lightly licking her clit while Jameson fucked her pussy. *Fuck, her pussy tastes so damn good; so sweet.*

I was gently nibbling and sucking on her clit while she continued sucking and licking her tongue on mine, causing me to holler out. All the while, my husband was banging the shit out of her pussy.

"Damn, you got some good pussy. That's it, fuck me back; nice and nasty, just like that."

"Si, that's so good how you are fucking me. Do not stop, I'm going to cum all over your dick."

Pulling his dick out of her soaking wet canal, Jameson started finger fucking her real good.

"Oh, Papi, Si, I'm going to fucking squirt all over you."

"Do it!" he ordered.

"Si, si, do not stop. Here it cummmmmms! Oh my God, si, si." she moaned.

While Gabriela continued to cum, Jameson stuck his dick back in her quivering pussy and started ramming the shit out of her pussy again.

"Oh, oh, oh, si, si, si."

"Gabby, I'm going to cum all in your mouth. Yes, suck it. Lick it just like that." I shouted. "Oh, oh yes, yesssssss."

"Oh, baby girl, I'm going to bust, bring me your mouth now!" Jameson ordered.

"Yes, give it to me, daddy."

Sticking his cock in my mouth, he began pumping furiously. "Oh shit, oh shit, that's what I'm talking about. Damn!" he said.

*****

We continued sucking and fucking one another all night. We had done so many positions, making sure to cum all over each other again and again. After finally exhausting ourselves, we decided to all take a shower together. One thing lead to another and it started all over again. We continued fucking one another until it was time to go.

This is the absolute best anniversary Jameson and I have had in a very long time.

Gabriela is now a permanent partner in our lives. We get together often and stay wet around each other.

Ridin' Dirty

"Clyde, you got to be in and out of this." I said.

"You're right, I got to be in and out of this pussy. Shit girl, you got that bomb shit, now spread them legs wider and stop acting like you scared to fuck."

"Clyde, my mom gets off work in an hour and if she catches us fucking in her house again, she just might kill us both."

"Jess you worry too much. Come on girl, let me bust this pussy wide open." he said with a knowing look.

Spreading my legs wide, I let him see just how wet my pussy was.

"Ah yes, look how wet you gettin."

"Shhhhhhh! Stop talking so much, boy, and fuck me."

Sliding between my legs, he rubbed his cock slowly along my clit. Ramming his dick deep inside me, he began fucking my soaking wet pussy.

"Yes, that's it, pump that dick all inside me." I moaned.

"Spread your lips apart, I wanna make sure I hit that clit right."

"Oh yes baby. Ah, ah, ah, you fuck me so good."

"Yes baby, whose pussy is this?" Clyde asks.

He knows this pussy belongs to him, but I answer him anyway. "It's yours, baby. This pussy is yours."

"That's right, baby, that pussy belongs to me." he says. "Now come down here and taste your juices on this dick."

"Oh baby, yes, let me taste that dick."

"That's right girl, suck this dick. Tilt that ass up real high so I can see it. Spread your legs so that asshole can breathe."

Sticking my ass up in the air, I spread my legs while continuing to suck his dick.

"That's it, baby, suck it. I love watching you slide your tongue around this dick.

Grabbing the back of my head he forced my head up and down his shaft in a steady rhythm.

"Pull them balls in your mouth. Ah yes, girl. Damn you sure know how to suck some dick. Shit, girl, you going to make me cum down your throat." he moaned

"Yes baby, cum down my throat. Gag me; pump your dick faster. Faster!" I shouted. "Mmmmmmmmm, that feels so fucking good, baby."

"Shit girl, turn that pussy around so I can suck your clit."

Before I could turn around and show him this pussy, he said, "Hold up, let me open this ass wide, I want to lick all this ass first.

Sitting back on his face, I started grinding my ass all over his tongue. *Damn! That feels so fucking good.*

"That's right, let me feel them juices running down my face."

"Oh baby, yes, suck this clit. Lick it, baby. Shit, you got me so wet. Yes! Clyde, you're going to make me cum!" I moaned.

"That's it girl, suck this dick. Let me bust all down your throat. That's it…swallow this dick.

Feeling his body tense, I knew it wouldn't be long before he was busting his load straight down my damn throat.

"Oh shit, Jess, here it comes."

"Mmmmm, mine too, baby! Oh yes. Clyde, suck it out of me. Yesssssssss! Shit, you eat my pussy so fucking good." I said breathlessly.

"Girl, take this dick. Suck it, that's it."

Feeling him force his cock further down my throat had my pussy juicing flowing.

"Swallow it, baby. I got some more cum in there. I want you to suck it all out of me, girl. Here it comes, baby. Oh shit! Yes girl, get it."

With a satisfied smile on my face, I lick my lips and look at Clyde. "We so nasty."

"You like this shit, girl. Now let's get the hell out of here before your mama gets back."

"You right."

Getting dressed and grabbing our stuff, we headed for the door. Before I closed the door Clyde shouted, "Hey, grab my weed."

"Alright baby, I'll get it." Grabbing his weed, I walked back toward the door. Now let's get out of here."

Jumping in the car, we sped off down the road. We had a big target to get to and we were running late. The cash was calling, and we were going to get ours.

*****

"Babe, roll that blunt for me so I can get my head straight."

"I got you, boy." I said as I was rolling a big fatty.

There is nothing like a heist that you're about to pull off; your adrenaline is pumping and you feel like you are on top of the world. Besides, my man looks so sexy when he is getting his bad boy on.

Arriving at the location of our mark, Clyde turns to me and says, "Okay girl, you ready? Grab my mask."

Grabbing his mask from the back, I handed it to him, "Here you go, baby. I'll be right here with the car running and when you get back, I'll ride that dick all the way back home."

"I'm gonna hold that ass to it! Okay, mama, let's do this. Give me seven minutes; if I'm not back, you get the hell out of here. You hear me?"

"Yes, baby, I hear you. You just get your ass back here."

Getting out of the car, Clyde headed to go collect our prize. *Shit, this is always the hardest part...waiting.*

It's not like we even have to do this shit, our parents are rich as fuck. We just like it. We are about fifty or sixty robberies in and we've not been caught yet. *And I'd like to keep it that way.*

*****

Two and half minutes: "Come on, baby. Get in and get out."

Four minutes: "Come on, baby, you can do it." *He'll be fine, he is always about two minutes shy of his time.*

Tapping my feet on the floorboard, I gripped the steering wheel tightly. The palms of my hands were sweating uncontrollably. *Fuck! My nerves are on edge.*

"Come on, baby. What are you doing?" Looking at the time, I realized his time is almost up.

Six minutes: "Shit! He has never taken this long. "Come on, Clyde, where you at baby?"

Fuck, something must be wrong.

"Don't do this to me; come on baby." *Fuck! Where is he at?*

Looking at the time, it began to sink in that I was going to have to ride out.

Seven minutes: "FUCK!" I shouted, tears filling my eyes. As I peeled out, speeding down the road, unable to see where I was going, I could not longer stop the tears from falling. Crying hysterically, I started thinking, *Why now? We never get caught. My life isn't complete without him.*

"Fuck this! I'm going back."

Just before I turned the car around I happened to look in my rearview mirror, and there he was, running down the street. Stopping the car, I slammed it in reverse and screeched all the way back to him.

As he jumped in, I yelled, "Fuck, babe, what the hell?"

Laughing, Clyde said, "I had to get in that vault, and baby girl, we hit the fucking jackpot on this one."

He was hugging me, while shaking me and kissing me, repeating how we had hit the fucking jackpot.

"Damn baby, you should have seen me. I was so damn pumped. Fuck, they won't know what hit them."

I was so happy that he was okay and that nothing went wrong. Seeing his smile while he told me about what happened had my pussy screaming.

"Switch me places, boy. That shit got my pussy on fire."

Slapping him playfully on the arm I tell him, "I thought I lost you. You can't do shit like that again, okay? I don't ever want to live without you."

"Girl, I'm fine, but I promise, you will never have to feel that way again. Now give me that wheel, pull that skirt all the way up and let me see you play with that clit."

Leaning back against the door, I spread my legs and gently began rubbing my clit. "Like this, baby?"

Banging on the wheel, Clyde says, "Hell yea, girl! Just like that. Slide that finger you were just playing with that pussy with, right here in my mouth."

Slipping my finger inside my wet pussy, I removed it, slipping it into my man's mouth.

Licking and sucking my finger, he gave a slight moan before saying, "Damn, that shit is sweet. Your pussy tastes good, babe. I'm ready for you to take a ride on this dick."

My pussy was dripping wet. "Me too, baby."

"Hold on, let me get this seat back a little." Sliding the seat back, to allow a little extra room, I carefully slid across and straddled his legs.

"Yes girl, slide that pussy hole right on your man."

Slipping my sloppy, wet hole over his cock, I pleaded, "Baby, please don't scare me like that again."

"I'm sorry, baby, I just wanted it to make sense; if this is our last one we had to go out big. Fuck, your pussy is tight." Moaning he said, "Ah, I like when you do that shit."

I knew exactly what shit he was talking about. Tightening my pussy around his cock, I asked, "What shit, baby?"

"That shit right there; when you flex your muscles on this dick. Oh shit, I'm about to bust. Oh shit baby, fuck, ride this dick, let me feel them juices drip all down my balls."

His cock felt so good inside me, I didn't think I was going to be able to hold out much longer.

"That's it, Jess, that's it. Hold on girl, I'm about to explode all in your pussy. Let me pull this shit over, get in the back and lie flat. I want to fuck that ass."

"Yes baby, I'm ready."

"Suck on this dick for a minute."

Taking his dick in my mouth, I sucked him all the way down. *Mmmmmmm, he tastes so damn good.*

"Oh shit, swallow that dick. Suck it, baby. You get me hard as hell."

"Baby, put it in my ass." I said, wiggling my ass back into him.

"Girl, you ready? That's it, baby, wiggle that ass back on this dick. Damn, that asshole is fucking tight as hell."

"Fuck me, Clyde! Ram that dick all in my ass, baby. Yes, yes, yes, hurt this ass." I moaned.

"Fuck this dick, girl. Let me play with that clit. Damn, your pussy is wet as hell, just like I like it. That's it, buck that ass, girl."

"Oh, oh, shit. Don't stop rubbing my clit. Rub it faster. Fuck my ass just like that."

"Girl, I can't hold on."

"Yessssss! I'm cummmmming, baby.

Grabbing hold of my hair he pulled on it before busting all up in my ass.

Collapsing on top of me, we laid there trying to catch our breath and regain our composure before heading home.

"Girl, we nasty. That's why I like ridin dirty with you. Let's get home and count this stash and plan our future."

Leaning over and kissing him, I said, "Yes, baby, let's ride."

OTHER BOOKS BY FELICIA LEWIS

LOVE & LUST EROTIC TALES

I felt my temperature rising between my thighs, my heart rate sped up. My breathing came in fast and short. My thoughts were spinning inside my soul, my breast heaved up and down. My nipples became erect from the anticipation of what was about to take place within my mind. I felt the stirring of my thoughts about to erupt. I placed my hand on my delicate flower and took myself on an ultimate high. He begged me not I told him I had too. Dive into some of the most erotic tales you will ever experience in your lifetime. Love & Lust Erotic Tales will have you creaming for more.

About Felicia Lewis

Instagram: porschaafterdark

Google Plus: Porscha After Dark

Twitter: @authorporscha

Facebook: www.facebook.com/flewis1985

You can contact Felicia Lewis at

porschaafterdark@outlook.com

Being from Pittsburgh, Pennsylvania, I have been through and have seen a lot. I read everything I could get my hands on at a young age. I began writing at the age of 13 years old. I always knew there was something different about me and I had a gift to share. I processed things differently in my mind. Teachers, elders, and people I had conversations with asked how I thought of such things. My response was, "My mind speaks for itself. I follow what it tells me to do and say." With that ability, I can creatively write for readers of all races, nationalities, and cultures to be captivated through my words.

Made in the USA
Columbia, SC
08 February 2019